The Cowboy's Prize

The Cowboy's Prize

A Sweethearts of the Rodeo Romance

Jamie K. Schmidt

The Cowboy's Prize

Tule Publishing First Printing, February 2024

The Tule Publishing, Inc.

First Publication by Tule Publishing 2024

Cover design by Llewellen Designs

ISBN: 978-1-961544-50-5

Prologue

Three years ago

LeAnn "Killer" Keller was hung over. But because she was almost nineteen, she couldn't tell her parents that. As far as they knew, she had been tucked in her bed last night, dreaming of winning the first gold belt buckle in the Women's Professional Rodeo Circuit of America's bronc-riding event. Instead, she had been attempting to shake her "America's Sweetheart" reputation by trying to attract the interest of rodeo bad boy Luke "Mick" Mickleson. Except Mick had only been interested in getting her drunk and trying to get into her pants.

Her older sister Reba, thankfully, had gone looking for her and had sat with her while LeAnn puked on her shoes and cried when Mick went home with Debbi Peterson instead.

Walking over to the vending area, LeAnn got a Coke and hoped that it would settle her stomach. She glared over at the barrel riders, laughing and cheering each other on. She used to be a barrel racer, a damned good one too. But she had stopped competing in that event so that she could concentrate on the new bronc-riding title.

Reba had cleaned her up and snuck her back into the

Winnebago they all lived in, without waking her parents. LeAnn owed her one. She owed all her sisters for putting up with her this year. Her parents were crazy overprotective and when LeAnn hit eighteen, she had let the freedom go to her head a bit.

She had three older sisters: Reba, Dolly, and Loretta. Her parents were huge fans of country-western singers. They named her and her sisters after legends in the business. Her oldest sister, Loretta, was back home in Paris, Texas, holding down the fort and going through a nasty divorce. But Dolly and Reba had been traveling with LeAnn and their parents to all of her rodeos for the last few years.

"You're lucky it was me and not Dolly who found you," Reba said to her this morning. It was true, too.

Reba was a veterinarian. It had been very handy to have her on the road. She'd had a hellacious experience at her last job. LeAnn still didn't know all the details, but Reba had felt threatened enough to quit a good-paying job to live in the Winnebago with them. It must've been pretty bad.

Dolly worked in public relations. This past year, she'd been working on building LeAnn's social media accounts and trying to leverage likes, clicks and other stuff into paying sponsors.

She had carefully crafted LeAnn into being the new face of the WPRC. So far it had gotten them some mid-range sponsors. But LeAnn needed to win this final competition to attract the really big dogs. She should have had it in the bag, but her rankings had slipped ever since her eighteenth birthday. Too many parties and too many late nights had allowed Merry Grayson to inch her way up to the number-two spot.

"You don't look so good," Dolly said, coming up to where LeAnn was grimly holding on to the fence while contemplating her poor decision to go out last night.

"I'm all right." LeAnn swallowed the acid burning in the back of her throat.

She dodged away from Dolly's hand on her forehead.

"You don't seem to be running a fever."

"I said I'm fine." All LeAnn wanted to do was curl up and sleep for a week. But she had less than a half hour before she rode her heart out in the saddle-bronc competition.

"Merry's on top of her game today. She's kicking ass in breakaway roping."

"Wonderful," LeAnn grumbled. She regretted giving up competing in all of the other rodeo events so she could concentrate on winning the saddle-bronc category.

Merry Grayson was tough to beat on a normal day. One half of the "Wild Grayson Sisters," Merry was a hell-raiser, an ass-kicker, and everything LeAnn secretly wished she had the balls to be. Instead, LeAnn had become an overprotected baby sister and a dutiful daughter who never talked back or broke the rules out of fear of being hauled back to Paris, Texas, and all those beauty pageants her mother insisted she compete in.

LeAnn had been pushing her luck with her parents, though, ever since she told them after being crowned Miss Texas Teen, that she'd rather be a barrel racer than a beauty contest queen. Her mother had been heartbroken. Her father had been relieved. But then all their enthusiasm shifted from pageants to rodeos. She felt like their pet project sometimes, instead of their daughter. Miss Texas Teen USA became Killer Keller.

Then LeAnn turned eighteen and the knowledge that her parents couldn't control her life was headier and more intoxicating than those tequila shots she had done last night.

Her stomach heaved at the thought of tequila.

"Maybe she'll be too tired from roping and barrel racing to put in a good day on the bronc," LeAnn said hopefully.

"Just do the best you can," Dolly said. "We're all rooting for you." With a quick squeeze, Dolly left her to her thoughts. She was probably off to take pictures for the WPRC's Instagram account or something.

LeAnn shook herself out of her funk and tossed her empty soda cup into the trash. She wandered over to where the bull riders were hanging out, waiting for their turn to test their skills against the ornery beasts. That was her next goal. Once she got the buckle for winning the bronc-riding event, she'd start practicing on bulls. It would only be a matter of time before the WPRC opened that category up for women to compete.

Craning her neck, she tried to see if Mick was around, but it didn't look like it. Instead, she was treated to another form of eye candy—Dylan Porter was tugging on leather gloves and strapping on his chest protector. His extra-wide chest protector. Dylan wasn't drop-dead gorgeous like Mick, but he had a sexy smile and warm bedroom eyes that captivated her, always had. She swooned at them the first time she saw him at the rodeo when she was sixteen and he was twenty-one. He hadn't paid her a lick of attention then, and now that she was old enough, LeAnn wasn't sure how to talk to someone like him. She must have been staring because he looked up and caught her ogling him.

"You all right, Killer?" he asked.

Dylan had a sexy drawl that made her shiver. She swallowed hard and nodded. Talking with him wasn't like talking with Mick. Dylan didn't flirt or tease. He treated her like a professional and like an athlete, but he looked at her like she was still a kid.

Except for that one time.

On her eighteenth birthday, her family had thrown her a surprise party at a local VFW hall in the rodeo town they were in. Mick had been there, but it was Dylan's slow once-over that had made LeAnn weak at the knees. She'd give anything to have him look at her like that again. LeAnn often thought about that dance and how safe and content she had felt while in Dylan's arms. But after one dance, Dylan had disappeared.

Mick had been more than happy to take up the slack, and he and LeAnn had been on again off again ever since. Mostly off again, because she was saving herself for marriage, and Mick thought that was a stupid idea.

"Good luck out there," she managed to say as Dylan dusted his hands off on his leather chaps.

"Don't need luck," he said. "I've got skill."

"Yeah," she said, feeling more confident. "Me too."

"Give 'em hell today." Dylan smiled at her, and she

wished he had been around last night. She might have drunk less and danced more.

She sat in the stands to watch him ride. He stayed on for eight seconds. Mick did not. That would put him in a hell of a mood tonight. It would serve Debbi Peterson right to have to deal with him sulking about losing at the after-party the rodeo was sponsoring. While Mick cried in his beer, LeAnn would be modeling her gold belt buckle for everyone to see.

And if she was lucky, maybe Dylan Porter would come up to her afterwards and ask her to dance.

SHE LOST.

LeAnn blinked back tears as she put Garth back into the barn for the night. Her body went through the motions of brushing and taking care of him. Inside though, she was sobbing like a little girl. She'd not only lost, she'd also gotten her ass handed to her. She didn't even place in the top three.

Merry took first. She took it all. Merry had won every event and not only took home the first women's bronc-busting gold belt buckle, she took home the all-around trophy, and fifty thousand dollars too.

LeAnn would be taking home a bunch of outstanding bills and a few "I told you so's" from her parents. Wiping tears away with the back of her hand, she finished with Garth and left the barn before her sisters—or worse, her parents—could come looking for her. She couldn't bear to attend the after-party and there was no way in hell she was going back to the Winnebago.

She drove her truck to a local bar instead and ordered up a tequila sunrise. It felt good going down, so she ordered another one, and another, until she no longer felt like crying. In fact, after three of them, all she felt was a nice, dazed buzz that made her forget her failure and disappointment.

A little voice in her head told her that she had only herself to blame. But she shoved that voice down deep and picked up a pool cue. She might not know how to ride a bronc, but she knew how to shoot a combo.

The next few hours passed in a blur. LeAnn wasn't sure when Mick showed up or why, but suddenly he was there, and just as quickly, she was riding in his truck with him. Then, flash forward, they were making out in the parking lot in front of the honky-tonk where the rodeo had the after-party. LeAnn was confused, but she decided to go with the flow. It was a celebration after all, right? Although, she wasn't sure why she was celebrating.

Mick's hands started getting more aggressive and warning bells sounded in the back of her head. But they were faint and far away. However, before things progressed any further, Debbi opened the truck door and pulled LeAnn out by her hair.

"Man-stealing bitch," Debbi snarled and threw a wild punch.

Even as drunk as LeAnn was, she dodged it and swayed when Mick grabbed Debbi and dragged her away.

"Bye!" LeAnn waved and slumped against Mick's truck.

What the hell was she doing?

Sliding down to the ground, LeAnn held her head and let go with the tears she had tried to wall up. It was an ugly, snotty cry and she hoped that no one was filming this on their phone. But then again, why would they? She was a loser. No one cared for the sixth-place rider, even if it was on a bronc in an event that never had a woman's champion before now.

"Are you all right, honey?" A man crouched down next to her.

Looking up, she saw Merry Grayson's face. Wait...how? Realization hit her and she staggered to her feet. The man was wearing a T-shirt that had Merry's smiling face on it. Just what she didn't need.

"I'm fine." LeAnn sidled away from the nightmare shirt. She wanted to punch Merry's perfect teeth out. And that wasn't fair. Merry hadn't done anything but ride better today. And the man wearing the T-shirt just had bad fashion sense.

"Can I call someone for you?" he asked.

"No." LeAnn put her hand up to shield herself from seeing Merry grinning at her. "I know I fucked up today."

"I'm sorry," the man said.

"You don't have to rub it in, Merry."

"Merry?" the man looked confused. "Oh, my T-shirt. Yeah, I'm a big fan of hers."

"Jackass," LeAnn snorted.

"Excuse me, little girl?" The man crossed his arms over his chest. "I think you've had too much to drink."

"I think I haven't had enough, if the party is filled with

people wearing Grayson merchandise," she said.

"Wait," he said, narrowing his eyes. "I know you."

"No, you don't." LeAnn shook her head. "No one does. Hell, I don't even know who I am anymore. I used to. I was the golden girl of the rodeo. I was going to be the next big thing."

"Let's get you inside and see if we can sober you up." He reached for her arm, but LeAnn shook him off.

"I don't need your help." She staggered away. "I don't need anyone's help."

But she did. Because she was not sure what the heck she was going to do now. She was looking at a long off-season back in Paris, Texas, where her family would try to convince her to get a "real job." The problem was, the thought of sitting in an office all day and only going to local rodeos on the weekends made her throat close up.

"How old are you?" the man asked.

"Old enough to know better and young enough not to care," she said. In fact, she was going to continue the party without Mick. There was a bar full of people who liked her. She took two steps and then swayed. Of course, Merry might be in there. Looking back at the man over her shoulder, she asked, "Is Merry in there?"

The man grinned and maybe blushed a little bit too. "She sure is. She signed my shirt." He pointed to the silver scrawl across his chest. "I've been a fan of her and her sister June since they started. They're pretty wild."

"You want to see wild?" LeAnn had just about enough of hearing about Merry and being wild. LeAnn had been a good girl. She'd followed the rules and where had it gotten her? Nowhere. Fumbling with her pants, she dropped them halfway down her thighs. Turning around she flashed her backside at the man. "Here's a full moon for you!"

"And that's about enough of that," the man said, waiting until she had buttoned up her Levi's before taking her by the upper arm.

"You let go of me, or I'll scream," she said.

"Go ahead and scream." He sounded bored as he marched her through the parking lot.

"I mean it. I'm calling the cops." LeAnn fumbled with her cell phone.

"Honey, I am the cops. Off duty. But you're going to sit in the drunk tank to sober up. If you behave, maybe I'll drop the indecent exposure charge."

Wasn't that crazy? Just when you thought your life couldn't suck any more, it suddenly did.

Chapter One

Three years later

LeAnn "Killer" Keller would have kicked open the door to the bar, but it was already open. She was too pissed off to cry. She needed a drink, and she needed one badly. Storming up to the bartender, LeAnn ordered a shot of tequila.

She and tequila had a history. LeAnn had made some bad decisions when she and tequila partied too hard. But tonight, she needed the sweet burn to wash away the grief and anger.

A whole year.

Mick had been cheating on her for their entire relationship.

And it was her fault.

LeAnn downed the shot before she realized she'd failed to ask for a name-brand tequila, and they had given her a drink from the well bottle. At least now she could blame her stinging eyes and the tears that threatened on the rotgut tequila she'd just guzzled, instead of on her broken heart.

"Another one. Cuervo Gold this time."

"You want some salt and lemon with that too?" the bartender asked.

"Why not?" she said, nodding.

Her phone hadn't stopped blowing up. Mick again. Like they hadn't just shouted at each other all through the barn and the rodeo arena until she got into her truck and nearly ran him over in the parking lot.

"Fuck him," she muttered, and then blocked his number.

Her phone buzzed again. This time it was her sister Dolly, asking her what the hell was going on.

LeAnn gave a watery snort and swiped her arm across her eyes. *Mick and I broke up. Don't want to talk about it,* she texted back.

But Dolly would want to talk about it. Ever since LeAnn blew her reputation as the WPRC's rodeo sweetheart three years ago, they had been scrambling for sponsors. This past year, Dolly had been working her ass off trying to rebuild LeAnn's status. It had helped that LeAnn was damned good at rodeo events, but social media had a long memory. There was still video of her drunk ass mooning the cop floating around. Dolly was having to work overtime to get sponsors to give her another chance to represent their brands. So far, no one wanted her.

No one had ever wanted her, except for Mick. And now that had been taken away from her, too.

Everything's a mess, she started to text to Dolly. Then deleted it…and turned off her phone.

Mick cheating on her was the rancid cherry on the shit sundae of her life.

Her parents had been disappointed in her ever since she'd spent the night in the drunk tank three years ago.

That had been the last straw for them. It had been bad enough that LeAnn risked her health riding bucking broncos instead of excelling at barrel racing, like she had been doing for most of her career. But after one loss, she fell apart? They had urged her to get out of the rodeo before it destroyed her. Her sisters had been more supportive, but she couldn't shake the feeling that they weren't too happy about not being on a winning team.

"We didn't raise you to go wild and disrespect authority figures," her parents often reminded her when they spoke on the phone to each other once a week.

No, they hadn't, and LeAnn had three long years to be ashamed of herself as she tried to work her way back. In her defense, she had just turned eighteen at the time, and had been hellbent on sowing all the wrong oats.

Her parents had stayed home after that nightmare season, but they begrudgingly let her and her sisters use the Winnebago to travel across the United States from rodeo to rodeo. She knew that a condition was that Dolly and Reba had to promise to keep an eye on her so she wouldn't embarrass herself—or them—again. So her sisters continued to travel with her as benevolent wardens in a Winnebago prison.

The bartender set her up with another shot glass. This time, LeAnn took a moment to appreciate the amber color and the sweet smell of the agave. Licking the top of her hand, she dusted it with salt. After coating her tongue with the salt, she slung back the tequila and then jammed a lemon slice into her mouth. Sucking on the sour juice, she remembered how much she liked the tart bite. It had gone down smooth, and the two shots were doing their job of numbing the pain.

"Another," she barked. "Please," she added as an afterthought.

He poured her another. And this time, her stomach jolted when she smelled the tequila. Maybe she should slow down.

"All alone tonight, Killer?" a voice drawled from the end of the bar.

It was early in the evening, so the bar wasn't too crowded, which was good because she didn't want to talk with anyone from the rodeo—especially anyone with a dick. But this was Dylan Porter. And even though he had a dick, he wasn't one.

LeAnn hadn't noticed him when she had come in, which might have been a first for her. She had always admired Dylan, as a bull rider and as a man. Even with her insides twisting and raging against all things male, she could appreciate the curve of his biceps against his black cotton shirt.

She'd always been drawn to him. He loved animals and treated his horse like gold. LeAnn used to watch him when he wasn't looking while he took care, not only of his horse, but he also made sure that all the horses in the barn were comfortable, well fed and watered.

He'd always have a special place in her heart for helping out Garth that time when his feed bucket had fallen and emptied out. Dylan had fixed it and made sure Garth had enough food to get through the night.

"Not just tonight," she said. "I'm all alone for good."

"You broke up with Mick?"

"What makes you think he didn't break up with me?" She took her tequila, salt, and lemon down to the end of the bar and sat down on a barstool next to him.

Dylan wasn't part of the crowd that hung out together after the rodeos, but sometimes he was there, playing pool in the bars Mick had smuggled her underage ass into when her sisters thought they were at the movies. She and Dylan had never hung out, but he wasn't one of the jerks who liked to make fun of the women riding broncs.

"Because even though Mick is an asshole, he's not stupid," Dylan said. "Only an idiot would let you get away."

His words and the admiring look in his eyes made her heart thump. It was warm in here, especially sitting so close to him. LeAnn stared down at their knees, almost touching.

"Then he's an idiot, as well as an asshole," she muttered.

"You mean to tell me that Mick broke up with you tonight?"

"He didn't actually say those words, but since he was banging a buckle bunny a half an hour ago, I took it to mean that that was goodbye."

Dylan winced. "I'm sorry, sweetheart. You didn't deserve that."

"Didn't I?" she said bitterly and tanked the shot, forgetting about the salt and lemon.

Mick had wanted sex and LeAnn had wanted to wait until marriage. That's what her parents had always taught her and her sisters. But lately, she had been starting to come around to Mick's point of view that there was no point in waiting. This year, they had started to date exclusively. And she had been planning to sleep with the bastard, even though there was still a part of her that wanted to wait.

Her head started to pound, and she felt sick. She went to signal the bartender for another one, but he was down the bar with another customer. Dylan took ahold of her outstretched hand and held it. "He ain't worth it."

His thumb caressed her knuckles. She deliberately moved her leg closer to his. LeAnn hadn't realized how much she craved physical contact that wasn't expected to turn sexual. And yet, something inside her buzzed at his nearness. LeAnn was pretty sure this wasn't the tequila talking.

"I know that now," she said. "But I just spent the last few years of my life trying to be everything he wanted. Well, almost everything." She gave a half-laugh.

It wasn't that she didn't want to have sex. She did. She just hadn't been sure if she wanted to have sex with Mick. And after all these months, LeAnn should have known the answer to that question. So she really couldn't blame him for fooling around. At least, that's what Debbi Peterson told anyone who would listen.

"You kept him waiting for all that time. What did you expect?" Debbi had said when she saw her crying tonight.

That had stung. There had been other girlfriends in between Debbi and LeAnn, though, so for some dumb reason, she had thought that Debbi would have been on her side.

"I had expected him to let me know if he wanted to

see—sleep with other people," LeAnn had said when she'd recovered from the verbal blow.

"You got too focused on riding," Debbi had said.

That part was true. LeAnn was trying to get back on top after a disastrous couple of years brought on by her partying too hard and the last few months trying to be the girlfriend that Mick wanted, to make up for not sleeping with him. LeAnn had dressed the way he said to, had followed him around to wherever he wanted to go, and had listened quietly to all the toxic male bullshit that he and his friends like to spew after they'd had a few beers.

The last part had been the worst. She hated herself for becoming "that girl," just to please him.

"I need to win," LeAnn had said to Debbi.

"You need to grow up," Debbi had told her. "You can't blame a man like Mick for not wanting to babysit you. Maybe if you had kept him satisfied, he wouldn't have had to sleep around."

Fortunately, LeAnn knew bullshit when she heard it. "Or he could have broken up with me and slept around all he wanted. He cheated because that's who he is." And part of her wondered who Debbi was, if she could defend him.

LeAnn and Mick had done other things, of course, aside from sex. She wasn't a nun. And it had been nice. Just not fireworks nice. She had been waiting for fireworks to happen, and she had said that to Debbi.

"That only happens in books and movies," Debbi had snorted.

They were barrel racers. They had both been wronged by the same man. Debbi should have had her back. That was the girl code, right? She should have grabbed a pitchfork and threatened to geld him or something. But instead, she'd taken Mick's side. And it had hurt like a bitch—a double betrayal that had left LeAnn reeling, and second-guessing herself.

"I'm an idiot too," LeAnn said to Dylan, who was still holding her hand.

"Not from where I'm sitting," he said.

"Mick told me what I wanted to hear. He said he respected my decision to wait until we got married to have sex. Did you know that he was sleeping with any sidepiece he could get his hands on, when I went back home after our dates?"

Mick had hit her with that awful fact when he had given up trying to talk his way out of the situation.

"I don't make it a point to follow what Mick does. But I'm not surprised."

"I was. That's why I'm an idiot. He said that he didn't mind waiting. That I was worth it. That he respected my decision. Of course, he didn't mind waiting—he was getting sex anytime he waved his dick around."

Dylan shook his head. "He's a liar and a fool. He talks a lot of shit and he's gotten his ass kicked more than once for it. He and I went toe-to-toe on a few things. He's got a face made for punching."

Her lips curved up in a reluctant smile. "If I wasn't giving him what he wanted, why did he stick around as long as he did?" Mick had said it was because he loved her. Love would have kept his dick in his pants, though.

"Because he knew a good thing when he saw it," Dylan

said, sipping a beer.

"Me?"

"You," Dylan said.

LeAnn wished she believed that. "I can't even win a barrel race anymore," she said miserably.

"Is that what you want to do?"

"I want to win."

"You've won buckles in barrel racing. I think you're looking for new challenges."

New challenges. New start. New everything.

"I think you could take first in the bronc category this year," Dylan said.

Hope filled her up, pushing out the grief. Her stats were good. She had busted her ass, determined to win and was on the right track, even if she had been slipping in rankings lately. LeAnn could let this thing with Mick screw her up or she could do what she should have done three years ago and put on her big girl panties and woman up to the challenge.

"You really think so?"

"Of course, you can," he said.

It was nice to get the positive reinforcement. Her parents wanted her to quit the rodeo. Dolly wanted her to stop bronc riding and devote all her time to barrel racing until everyone forgot Killer Keller was a fuckup.

"You had it all, when you were winning the barrel-racing events," Dolly said, thinking she was helping.

She hadn't been.

"You haven't won the bronc event yet. What makes you think you're going to?" her father would ask.

"You're spending too much time on the broncs," her mother would chime in. "If you don't start winning some events, you're not going to be able to afford gas."

That wasn't strictly true. She still had some savings from her big wins from previous years. Unfortunately, the pandemic had put a huge dent in her finances. No rodeos meant no prize money. LeAnn had coasted for a few years, but this year was literally a go-big or go-home moment for her. And it looked like she'd be going home to Paris, Texas, at the end of the rodeo season this year.

Panic seized her at that thought. She did not want to go home. Not at the end of the season. Not when she'd failed to live her dream.

"I feel like my life is so out of control right now. I can't win an event. My parents are on my case because of the bronc riding, and my sisters and I are together twenty-four seven in a Winnebago. At least when the season ends, they'll go home and maybe I can catch a break."

"What are you going to do in the off-season?"

"I need some space. I've got a couple of friends who could use some help on their ranches. I may go to a rodeo school to get more training. I definitely need more practice on broncs. I've let Mick and my social life get in the way of my career. I've got no one to blame for my latest bad scores, but myself."

"The season ain't over yet, Killer."

LeAnn gripped the end of the bar hard enough to make her knuckles turn white. "I want to win that bronc category so bad I can taste it."

"I've seen you ride. You can do anything that you want to do."

She had to take a few minutes to process that. Dylan seemed content to watch her work through this. And she was content to let him hold her hand while she noticed the slight stubble on his strong jawline. She wondered idly if it would tickle her neck or be scratchy. Her breathing quickened.

"You're good for my ego," she said, looking away, feeling shy and self-conscious all of a sudden.

Some of the men in the Men's Professional Rodeo Circuit of America weren't as supportive as Dylan. LeAnn didn't know why it was any of their business. The men had their own organization and the women had theirs. Aside from doing joint events every now and then, they had separate athletes, both two-legged and four-legged, separate rankings, and for the most part, different fans. The men's group also had a bigger budget and got more television time, but LeAnn didn't care. She liked competing against her peers in a more local setting. It felt more real. She wasn't a TV star. She was a rodeo queen, and damned proud of it.

"Women have no business on broncs," Mick had told her a few weeks ago. LeAnn wondered if that had been the beginning of the end. Or if it had been over long before that.

"It's boring to watch," another male bull rider had agreed with him when they had been hanging out at another generic bar after a rodeo that both organizations had promoted.

"It's a novelty," another one had chimed in. "It won't even be an event next year."

"I still beat your score," LeAnn had told him, speaking up for the first time in defense of herself and her sport. What had taken her so long?

That had led to a lot of spluttering and mansplaining.

"You had an easier horse."

"You get our rejects."

"The judges go easier on the women."

There wasn't any arguing with them, but LeAnn still tried. It was exhausting, always trying to prove herself.

"You've taken a few kicks in the gut, but you're a fighter," Dylan said, bringing her thoughts back to the here and now. "That's why they call you Killer."

His words were better than the tequila. And the admiration in his dark eyes went to her head like a downed shot. Suddenly she didn't want his thumb caressing her knuckles. She wanted his hands on other parts of her body. She shifted in her seat, as another flood of warmth filled her. A traitorous thought flitted through her. If Dylan had been her boyfriend, she wouldn't have lasted a year before deciding that waiting until she was married wasn't what she really wanted to do.

"I just have to get my head back in the game," LeAnn said. She had to get her whole body into the game. She needed to make some changes in her life. She needed to do things her way, find her own path. She wasn't going to be WPRC's sweetheart anymore. That ship had sailed. But it didn't mean it was the only ship in town. She just had to find out where she fit into all of this. She wasn't a Wild Grayson Sister, and she wasn't America's sweetheart. She wasn't just a daughter or a sister. And she sure as hell wasn't Mick's girlfriend.

So who was she?

She was a bronc rider.

"I'm going to win my next event." That was a good of a place to start. That meant no more tequila or wallowing in self-pity. She pushed her glass away from her.

"Now, you're talking." Dylan saluted her with his beer bottle. "Liam, put the lady's drinks on my tab."

"You don't have to do that," LeAnn said.

"I want to."

"Thanks." Impulsively, she braced a hand on his shoulder and leaned in to give him a kiss.

She probably should have kissed him on the cheek. But before she could think about it, she brushed her lips against his.

Sparks.

Opening her eyes wide, she stared at him. He looked just as surprised as she did. So she did it again.

More sparks.

The third time, she wrapped her arms around his neck and brushed her tongue against his. Slowly, he kissed her until she was half in his lap and breathless. It wasn't quite fireworks, not yet, but she was having a hard time pulling away from him.

"Sweetheart," he said hoarsely. "You don't want to do this."

But she did. LeAnn didn't want to talk anymore. She wanted to have sex with Dylan. She was more sure about that than she ever had been with Mick. Sure, it might have been the tequila influencing the decision. It might have roots as being just a revenge fuck. But she knew that that wasn't entirely what it was. LeAnn wanted to take this next step in her life.

She felt safe with Dylan, loved being this close to him. Eyes half-closed, she wondered what it would be like to be pressed up against a barn, legs wrapped around his waist while he pounded into her.

That's how she had caught Mick and the blond buckle bunny.

She let out a shuddering breath.

"You okay, Killer?" Dylan asked, concerned.

"I think I'm better than I've been in a long time," she said, slowly opening her eyes. The hateful image of Mick cheating on her had been replaced with a fantasy of her and Dylan.

"Good," he said. "You're better off without Mick." He trailed his fingers down her cheek and she leaned into the caress.

"I can see that now. I wasted so much time."

"Let go of the past. You can't change it. Concentrate on the now and what you want for the future."

Those were damn fine words. He was right. It was time to start over. She was going to be a new LeAnn who didn't care what the toxic cowboys thought. There was going to be a new commitment to excellence and success. She was going to rock the rest of the season.

And she was going to lose her virginity.

Tonight.

With Dylan.

"What do you say? Want to get out of here?" LeAnn

said, nuzzling his ear.

"Do you know where this will wind up if we do?" he asked, resting his hand on the small of her back. "Be sure this is what you want. No regrets."

"I've been a good girl since the day I was born and look where it's gotten me," LeAnn said. "I spent the last four years trying to get back my Goody Two-shoes reputation. I've been ridiculed by lots of people for riding a bronc. I've had to fight my parents for every ounce of independence. I spent the last year with Mick doing everything in my power not to sleep with him. That should have told me he wasn't the one."

"What's changed?" Dylan asked.

"I have. Now pay the tab and take me back to your hotel room."

For a terrible moment, she thought he was going to turn her down.

But then a wide smile spread across his face. "Yes, ma'am," he said.

Chapter Two

DYLAN FIGURED THEY'D go back to his hotel room, kiss and fool around for a bit and when LeAnn got cold feet, he'd offer her a drink and then drive her home. But he had sorely misjudged her determination to get laid.

The hotel room door had barely closed when she was kicking off her boots and pulling her shirt over her head.

"Whoa," he said, stopping her as she was about to shimmy out of her jeans.

"What's wrong?" she asked, looking unsure of herself.

"Slow down, sweetheart. We have all night."

Wincing, she said, "Actually, we probably only have a few hours. Otherwise, my sisters are going to come looking for me, and they can be pretty relentless."

"Give them a call and tell them where you are."

LeAnn was already shaking her head. "They're really overprotective. Not as bad as my parents were, but I don't want to deal with them tonight."

He stroked a finger down her cheek. "We don't have to do anything if you're getting cold feet."

"It is a little chilly in here," she said, looking uncertain for the first time. She sat down on the bed and stared at the floor.

"I can turn up the heat." He fiddled with the thermostat. She looked so pretty in her bra, but Dylan didn't want her to be cold. And as much as he wanted her, he didn't want to take advantage of her vulnerability. "Do you want to put your shirt on and we can go grab a cup of coffee?"

"Do you not want to have sex with me?" LeAnn asked.

Talk about trick questions. He sat down next to her on the bed. "More than anything. But it doesn't have to be tonight."

There was something about her that called to him, had always called to him since she'd been eighteen and had danced like a dream in his arms. She had been a talented kid, an upcoming rodeo star. But then, all of a sudden, she was a grown woman, beautiful and desirable. It had been a little disorientating, and he had felt odd having sexual thoughts about her after knowing her when she was younger.

Dylan had left her eighteenth birthday party early before he did something he'd regret. But after a few weeks, he had realized he wouldn't regret anything. LeAnn was legally an adult and only five years younger than him, so he got over his fear about robbing the cradle real quick, but not quick enough to save her from having to deal with that asshole Mickleson. He wouldn't have minded waiting until she was ready. Unlike Mick, he wanted more than just a romp between the sheets.

"No, it does," she said. "It absolutely has to be tonight."

Quicker than he would have expected, LeAnn straddled him and pushed his shoulders to the bed. He had just gotten pinned by a woman who was half his size. But he wasn't complaining. The view was gorgeous, and she fit nicely on his cock that was pressing relentlessly against his jeans.

"I don't want to talk anymore," she said, bracing herself on his shoulders as she leaned over him. "All I do is talk. It's time for action."

Dylan was confused and turned on in equal measures. Women didn't wind up in his hotel room and demand sex. You read about that in magazines and watched it on porn sites, but it never happened in real life. So this couldn't be real. Not that he was complaining. And if it had been anyone but LeAnn Keller, they'd already be under way.

While she had caught his attention on her eighteenth birthday, beautiful and tough in equal measures, LeAnn always had been a force to be reckoned with, both on and off her horse. He had wanted to get to know her better, but if she hadn't been with Mick, she had been with her family. Family and Dylan didn't go together. In fact, long-term relationships and Dylan didn't fit either. She should know that before this went any further.

"Sweetheart, I'm not boyfriend material."

He didn't have a "real job." He traveled from rodeo to rodeo all over the United States. His savings account was nonexistent and if he didn't win an event and collect his prize money, he slept in his truck.

"I had a boyfriend," she said. "I don't want another one."

"You say that now," he said, trying to do the right thing for once in his life.

"Dylan, do you want to fuck me or not?" She crossed her arms over her breasts, and he missed the view. Why was he fighting this so hard?

"Why me, Killer?" he asked. "And why tonight?"

"I want you," she said simply. "I have for a long time."

And just like that, he was all in.

Unhooking her bra, Dylan helped her slide it down her arms. Her breasts fit into his palms perfectly. LeAnn arched into his caress, moaned as he thumbed her tight nipples. He could spend hours just watching her reactions as he touched her. Dylan wanted hours, not a rushed grope session, but she was on a timetable. Flipping them, he pressed his mouth to hers for another one of those tequila-tasting kisses. This time, however, all he tasted was her, and it was everything.

Her fingers tangled in his hair as their mouths danced slowly over each other. She tugged at his shirt, and he lost a few buttons while taking it off. When they were skin on skin, he wanted more. Their jeans came off next and her soft, smooth body made him desperate to be inside her. But not yet. He knew this was her first time. How could he not know with Mick bragging about how he was going to bust LeAnn's cherry? Dylan had busted Mick's mouth instead.

But he wasn't going to think about that asshole right now. Not when LeAnn was on fire in his arms. He didn't want to stop kissing her, but he needed to feel her come against him. Reaching between their bodies, he dipped a finger between her legs.

Her mouth opened under his when he stroked through her wet folds. Her found her tight bud and circled it slowly, teasing the nerve endings. LeAnn reared her head back, filling the motel room with a deep moan. Dylan took the opportunity to clasp her pert nipple in his mouth and suck on it, while teasing it with his tongue.

Crying out, she bucked against his hand. He lavished attention on her lovely breasts while he fingered her until she writhed next to him. She dug half-moons into his shoulder with her nails as she shook apart.

Perfect. She was as perfect as he had imagined she would be. Kissing down her chest, to her belly, he licked her navel before hoisting her thighs on his shoulders.

"Dylan," she sighed.

He liked hearing his name on her kiss-swollen mouth. He liked tasting her even more. As he lapped her sweetness, he watched her pretty blue eyes widen when she realized she was going to come again.

Licking her fast, he gave a feral growl when her thighs trembled against his cheeks. She bucked and moaned, her fingers gripping the bedsheets. LeAnn rode his face as the orgasm tremored through her. She was still shaking and moaning as he took his time kissing his way up her body.

He was close to exploding, but he wanted this to be special for her. Wrapping her hand around his cock, he encouraged her to stroke him. He came almost immediately in her hand. That should give him enough of a respite to make her first time last longer than a few pumps and grunts.

"You're so sweet," he said, kissing her breasts again.

"Dylan," she said, her breath hitching. "I've never felt like this."

"I know," he said, and inserted a finger inside her. He leaned up on his arm and watched her eyes as he fucked her with it. When she moved to the rhythm, he put in a second finger. "Do you like that?" he asked silkily, nibbling on her neck.

"Yeah," she said, lifting her hips.

"I'm going to put a condom on and fuck you now," he said, pulling back to watch her eyes. "You can stop me if you want."

"Why would I do that?" She arched into his fingers as he pumped them inside her. Clamping down on him, LeAnn gave a little groan. "I need more."

"Be right there," he said. Reluctantly, he eased out of her.

She pouted and kneeled up to spread kisses over his shoulder and back while he dug the condoms out of his bedside table. His entire body was shaking with the effort not to fuck her hard and rough. When he got the condom on, he turned to her and kissed her until she was trembling in his arms. Placing her gently on her back, he eased inside her. She fit him tight, and his arms locked against the need to thrust deep.

"LeAnn," he groaned as she wiggled.

She looked up at him with trust and sleepy desire, and he forced himself to move slowly.

"Does it hurt?" he rasped out.

"Not really. It's tight though. Don't stop." She tugged on his hair.

"Just need a moment," he said, pushing fully inside her.

LeAnn gasped.

He kissed her again until her body melted against him.

Then she was like a wild thing. Her hands were all over his back and shoulders. Her legs wrapped around his and she wiggled and moved. His willpower broke and he pumped into her with increasing speed.

"Yes," she cried out, laughing.

He rode her long and hard, feeling her quiver and come underneath him. Just when he thought he'd explode inside her, Dylan flipped them so she was on top. He had slid out of her, and LeAnn was desperate to push him back inside.

"Let me help," he said guiding his cock up and in when she straddled him.

"Oh," she said, her eyes wide.

"Hey, beautiful," he said.

"Hey, yourself." She took in a shaky breath.

"Make yourself come."

"How?"

"Anyway, you want."

It took her a few tries to get the rhythm and speed down, but soon she was riding him hard, moving toward her own pleasure. Dylan was breathless and a second behind her. This was everything he had fantasized about since dancing with her at her eighteenth birthday.

Joy and desire lit up her eyes and LeAnn clenched tight around him. Dylan exploded, gripping her hips to keep her joined to him as he came. Afterwards, she sank down next to him.

"What time is it?" she muttered.

Dylan flopped his head toward the bedside clock. "Nine."

"I've got another hour," she said before kissing him hard.

Chapter Three

Six months later

LEANN STARED UP at the bright Texas sun. The fluffy clouds drifted lazily across her vision. The blue of the sky was so pure, her eyes watered. She felt dizzy and out of sorts.

"Get up!"

The ground trembled. Earthquake? LeAnn wasn't sure, but she rolled over on her hands and knees and forced her head up. It hurt.

Coming straight at her was an angry bull. He had horns that had been filed down, but that didn't lessen the terror that flooded through her at the sight of the animal coming toward her. It all came back to her now. She had wrecked. Gotten tossed off him, landed on his back hard, and then hit the ground. And this bull was one of the smaller ones she had been training with.

Adrenaline pushed her to her feet. Her helmet was askew. Her vest was tight and cutting into her, but she managed to dodge the bull's head as it swung at her. Stumbling back, LeAnn also avoided the bull's kicking back feet.

One of the bullfighters got in between the bull and her.

Another one slung an arm around her shoulders and hustled her out of the practice arena and safely behind the fence.

"You all right?" the bullfighter asked.

She managed a nod, but she was still feeling a little woozy and it was hard to catch her breath. LeAnn leaned against the fence and tried to look nonchalant. It was good practice for a real rodeo. In a real rodeo, though, she should have waved to the crowd. Right now, LeAnn wasn't sure she could do that without falling over.

The bullfighter returned to the arena to help set up for the next bull rider who was training at Trent Campbell's rodeo school. It took watching a few more rides and a lot of deep breaths for LeAnn to feel back to normal again. Taking a quick look around the stands, she was relieved that her family hadn't seen her get thrown. They didn't know she was practicing bull riding. It had been bad enough when they learned she was going to ride broncs.

They thought she was practicing barrel racing—not bull riding. LeAnn hated to lie to them, but she didn't want them to worry. She also didn't want to hear the same lectures they gave her when she told them she was going to bust broncs on the circuit.

"It's too dangerous."

"You can't control an animal like that."

"You're going to get killed."

"If you don't get killed, you'll have a career-ending injury."

They came around to that. They'd come around to this.

Eventually.

She hoped.

Bull riding was the next big event that the Women's Professional Rodeo Circuit of America was going to introduce—at least according to the rumors. And LeAnn was determined to dominate, right from the start.

Out of the corner of her eye, she saw Trent Campbell wandering over to her. She hid a grimace. He hadn't wanted to train her against her parents' wishes, but as she had told him, she was twenty-two and it didn't matter what they thought. LeAnn got the impression that he hadn't really wanted to train her because she was a woman, but he never came outright and said that. And to be fair, once she started training with him during the rodeo circuit's off-season, he hadn't treated her any differently than his other students.

The other men, on the other hand, had plenty to say about it. Some of them were just concerned that a "pretty little girl like her was going to get seriously hurt." Some of them thought she should go make them a sandwich, because women didn't belong in the rodeo. And a few didn't care one way or another, as long as she didn't get special treatment. She liked the last type better, but it hadn't made the past three months a whole lot of fun.

"What did you do wrong?" Trent asked as he came up alongside her.

Squinting at the bull rider in the arena, staying on a full eight seconds, LeAnn compared his ride to hers. "My knees weren't secure around the bull."

"And?"

LeAnn blew out a breath. "My upper body was too tight." She twisted back and forth to relieve her taut muscles. She was going to be sore and bruised tomorrow.

"It didn't help that Minotaur was in one hell of a mood today." Trent clapped her on the shoulder.

She did her best not to wince.

"Shit. Sorry. Do you need to see a doctor?"

"No," LeAnn said. "I didn't dislocate it or anything. I just landed on it wrong."

"Are you done for the day?"

LeAnn thought about it. She really wanted to be. But if the rumors were true, the WPRC was going to announce their new event soon. And LeAnn needed all the practice she could get if she was going to win the grand prize for being the first female bull-rider champion in WPRC history. The grand prize was a gold belt buckle and fat purse of one hundred thousand dollars.

The win would give LeAnn enough notoriety that she could attract some big-name sponsors. Even after the winning season she had just come off of, the sponsors were still a little gun-shy about hiring her to represent their brands. The problem was that they still thought of her as a disgraced rodeo princess instead of the damned fine athlete she was. LeAnn hated the uphill climb of getting her reputation back, but she was willing to put in the hours.

"I've got a few more in me," she told Trent as she dusted herself off.

"Just don't push it. I don't want you headed out to the first rodeo of the season hurt."

"Don't worry about me," LeAnn said. "I got this."

"If you're sure you can go another round, you're going to be on Apis," Trent said.

LeAnn scowled. "Apis is a muley and hardly even kicks."

"That's right, because you need to concentrate on your form. Give me any more lip and you can ride the mechanicals for the rest of the day."

LeAnn bit back her retort and resigned herself to getting on the hornless bull with a disposition that was almost sweet—comparably speaking.

Trent was a good riding instructor. He had built his bull-riding school on the Three Sisters Ranch in Last Stand, Texas. Over the years, he had expanded into teaching all rodeo events, bringing on June Grayson—the other Wild Grayson Sister—to teach barrel racing. It had been four years since LeAnn had had to compete against a Grayson sister, and she couldn't say she missed the experience. She liked them well enough outside of the arena, but inside they had been tough competitors and very hard to beat.

In the months following her loss to Merry all those years ago, she had partied hard to avoid thinking about what that loss had meant to her. She'd stayed out late, learned how to drink, and got involved with a crowd that was more about partying after the rodeo than the rodeo itself. But she had wrested back control of her life after breaking up with Mick last season.

And after that, it seemed like the rodeo gods had smiled on her. Or maybe it had been Dylan encouraging her to take back control of her career. LeAnn had won the women's bronc-busting championship for the first time. Before that, the best she had gotten was second place. It had taken all her effort in the last few months of the rodeo to pull it off.

She had been proud of her second-place showings as well, but as her ex-boyfriend liked to say to her, "Second place is first loser." She hated that she still allowed Mick to rent space in her head. She was working on evicting the sad son of a bitch, but for the moment, every nasty thing that she said or thought about herself sounded like it came straight from his mouth.

"It's just eight seconds," LeAnn muttered to herself as she settled on the bull in the bucking chute. She could do it on the smaller bulls like Apis and Minotaur. But she was having a harder time with the larger ones. Still, she assured herself that she just needed more practice.

Fastening the rope around her hand, LeAnn steadied her grip before giving the gate man a nod. He opened the gate, and Apis jerked out of the chute. She kept her knees tight and her upper body loose. When Apis spun left, she balanced out by leaning right. He danced up a bit and surprised her with a few back kicks and then the buzzer went off. Easing her hand out of the rope, she slid off the bull into a controlled jump and landed on her feet. Apis stormed around the arena for a few more seconds but didn't pay her any mind.

"Better," Trent said, clapping his hands.

"LeAnn Keller, just what the hell do you think you're doing?"

Oh shit.

"Excuse me," Trent said, and dipped his hat at her sister Dolly while he made a fast getaway.

"You can't put this on Instagram," LeAnn said. She wasn't ready to tell her parents about competing. She wanted to wait to have that argument once the WPRC made it an official event.

"Are you trying to get killed?" Dolly looked ready to strangle her.

"Would I be wearing protective equipment if I was?" LeAnn gestured at her padded vest and helmet.

Dolly just shook her head. "Why are you doing this?"

"You know why." LeAnn didn't have to tell Dolly any of the rodeo gossip. If Dolly didn't know about it, then it wasn't worth knowing. She had contacts all over the circuit and probably had known about the bull-riding event even before LeAnn had.

"You don't need a gold buckle that badly," Dolly said.

"You don't get to tell me what I need," LeAnn snapped, but at Dolly's hurt look, she immediately felt awful. They had been living in each other's back pockets for far too long and it was easy to become snippy. She and Reba should have gone home to Paris, Texas, instead of remaining with her in the Winnebago at a trailer park in Whiskey Creek. They all needed a break from each other.

Was it wrong that LeAnn just wanted to be first at something? Her three sisters always did things before she did, being older and not as pampered as LeAnn had been. She felt like she was constantly playing catch-up to them.

Loretta had been the first to move out of the house and get married. Reba had been the first to go to college. Dolly had been the first to become famous. She had been a Dallas Cowboys cheerleader. What had LeAnn done?

Her parents had sacrificed their retirement savings to buy a Winnebago so she could travel around the country to fulfill her dream of being a rodeo star, but she never broke a record or did anything that set her apart.

And while her sponsors and her prize money kept the family afloat, the past couple years had been tough when many venues had closed because of the pandemic. LeAnn felt that she was more of a drag on the family than a productive member.

"I'm sorry," LeAnn said. "I didn't mean that like it came out. Yes, I want to win a new event. And I really want the prize money. But I also want the sponsors that could come with that big win."

Dolly bit her lip. LeAnn knew she couldn't argue with that. "No one wants you to risk your life for that."

"I love the risks," LeAnn said simply. "I'm happy riding broncs and bulls."

"I'm telling Garth on you," Dolly said.

"He'll always be my heart, and he knows that, which is why we still kick ass." Garth was her barrel-racing horse and her best friend. Garth had been there for her without judgment when Mick had broken her heart. He hadn't said I told you so and hadn't shaken his head in sympathy. He'd just let her hug him and cry.

"Can't you just keep barrel racing and riding broncs?"

"You tell me," LeAnn challenged. "Has Lila Rogers returned your calls?" Lila was one of the top designers for Cowgirl Couture.

"Not yet," Dolly hedged.

"What about Sierra Drift boots?"

Dolly rolled her eyes.

"I'm grateful to the sponsors you've gotten for me. But if I'm going to make a career out of this, I need more than just the prize money."

"I get that," Dolly said. "And I'm trying."

"I know you are. I'm not complaining." LeAnn sighed.

"You're just so young and I'm worried that you're wasting your time with this."

LeAnn wanted to bang her head against the barn wall. "I'm twenty-two. When you were my age, you were living in Dallas in a shitty apartment trying to make ends meet by working all sorts of jobs, in between cheerleading."

"Talk about wasting time," Dolly said. Her forced smile looked more like a grimace.

LeAnn gripped her shoulders. "You lived your dream."

"And now the dream is over and I'm back in reality. I don't want you to have to struggle like I did." Dolly gently broke out of LeAnn's grip and turned away. She rubbed her arms as if she was cold.

LeAnn had always wondered about that time after Dolly had been cut from the team. LeAnn had been on the road with her parents, and hadn't been aware that Dolly had been struggling. When Dolly finally came back home to Paris, there had been shadows in her eyes, and it had taken a long time for the haunted expression on her face to go away. They didn't talk about what had happened. Not ever. And LeAnn wondered if maybe it was time.

"Dolly..." she said.

"Forget it." Dolly waved her hand. "It's nothing. I'm just concerned about you."

"I'm still living my dream," LeAnn said instead. "And I keep dreaming up more things. Like being the first woman bull-riding champion."

"And then what?" Dolly asked sadly.

"I'll find something else. But right now, this is what I'm going to do."

"When's it going to end?" Dolly asked. "Are you going to jump out of planes next?"

LeAnn didn't have the heart to tell her that was on her bucket list of things to do. "I need you to keep this a secret from Mom and Dad."

"You want to be an adult, but you're too afraid to tell them what you're doing?"

"I'll tell them myself," LeAnn said, feeling defensive. "I want to get some more practice and training under my belt so when the WPRC announces the event, I can ease Mom and Dad's minds that this is the right thing for me to do. Then when I win it all, I can send them enough money that they don't have to worry about retirement or anything else."

"I'm sure they'll find something to worry about. But I'll keep your secret," Dolly said reluctantly.

"Thank you." LeAnn hugged her hard.

"On one condition." Dolly squirmed free.

Oh crap.

"What?"

"I'm going to set you up with a trainer while you're on the road with the Texas rodeos. He'll be competing in the men's events as a bull rider, but he freelances on the side. You should be able to connect with him after hours to practice. He's a good guy. His name is Dylan Porter. He's not cheap, but we've got money in the budget to pay him, thanks to your big win last season."

"Dylan…Porter?" LeAnn said, her heart sinking. Her mind flitted back to that night and his sexy smile and smoldering eyes.

"Is there a problem?" Dolly pinned her with a glare.

"No. No problem."

Not one that she was going to tell her sister about anyway.

"Do you know him?"

LeAnn tamped down on the hysterical giggle that almost threatened to erupt.

He took my V-card in the wildest one-night stand I had ever.

"We've met."

And then I ghosted him because I was so damned embarrassed about how I acted.

Although, Dylan hadn't tried all that hard to reconnect with her either, so maybe he had been content to keep it as a one-and-done sort of thing. While that had depressed her, LeAnn hadn't let it distract her from training and working the competition. In the end, it was probably for the best she hadn't chased after Dylan and had concentrated on winning. Still, the thought of seeing him again brought up all sorts of confusing emotions.

"He's a good coach and a winning bull rider. I think you'll get along just fine."

If I can keep myself from tossing him on the bed and riding him for eight seconds. LeAnn felt herself blush at the image. She fought off a cringe at how rushed it had all been because she had wanted to get back to the Winnebago before her sisters found out about Mick and ruined her evening by calling until she picked up. It had been her first time, but looking back on it, LeAnn wished she could have handled the evening with more dignity and maturity. Maybe it was for the best that they hadn't had a chance to hook up again. It probably wouldn't compare to her heated memories anyway.

"I'm looking forward to working with him," LeAnn said. But first, she had to practice apologizing for running off and hiding like a scaredy-cat instead of facing him when she wasn't pissed off about Mick and full of liquid courage.

Chapter Four

DYLAN PORTER WASN'T sure if he wanted to get laid, get into a fight or just get a beer. Of course, all three weren't out of the question. He started out with the beer, sitting down at the bar. Swiveling his seat around so he could watch the pool tables, Dylan regarded his fellow bar patrons.

As far as fights went, a prime candidate was Luke "Mick" Mickleson. A fellow bull rider, Mick was a flaming asshole normally, but after a few drinks, his face became a magnet for fists. If Dylan didn't take his shot now, he might have to get in line. Currently, Mick was taking turns talking politics and religion, and well, he wasn't particularly receptive to opposing views.

Today had been rough. Johnny Montana's parents had been in the stands, watching Bobby—Johnny's younger brother. They had booed Dylan when it was his turn on the bull, and Dylan couldn't blame them. But then Johnny's father had thrown a beer bottle at Dylan and caught him in the back. Security had escorted the man out. Dylan was just glad his aim hadn't been better—he could have gotten him in the head. Still, it had shaken him and he'd ridden like crap today.

He could have used a win. It wasn't a big prize, but the five hundred would have paid for gas and his hotel room, and more importantly, his bar tab. Draining his beer in a few long swallows, he plunked the bottle down on the bar top with authority.

He was about to walk on over and give Mick the first shot, but then Dylan's phone rang. It was an unknown number, so he probably should just ignore it. But as his finger hovered over the decline button, at the last minute he decided to answer it. It might be Johnny's parents or Bobby, and he owed it to them to take the call. After all, it was his fault Johnny was dead.

"Yeah?" he challenged.

"Dylan? This is Dolly Keller."

Easing back into the barstool, he signaled the bartender for another beer. The phone call promised to be entertaining at least. "I am still not interested in posing for your shirtless bull-rider calendar." He was, however, still interested in Dolly's baby sister. But that was something Dolly wouldn't want to hear.

"Your loss. It's guaranteed money."

Dylan grunted. He wasn't that desperate yet. Although, if the medication that the vet put his horse Lola on didn't start working soon, he might be. He also needed to scratch together more money if he wanted to get taken seriously for the mortgage he was planning to apply for. He had his eye on a farm that was coming up on auction. If he was able to snag it, it would give Lola somewhere to retire to. And then once that was settled, Dylan could start on his own retirement project—opening a horse rescue for rodeo horses past their prime along with other unwanted animals. His business plan was top notch. It ought to have been. He'd been working on it for the last three years.

"But speaking of money," Dolly said. "Are you still offering bull-riding coaching while you're on the circuit?"

Was he? He flashed back to the grief he saw on Johnny's father's face today. Dylan wasn't sure he was up to taking on another student so soon after Johnny's death. But there were bills to pay and it would be nice to rent a hotel room instead of sleeping in his truck this season.

"Do I get to keep my shirt on?" he drawled.

"It's a requirement. Yes."

It was a damned miracle that anyone wanted him to coach them anymore. Officially, he wasn't to blame for Johnny's death last season. Unofficially, people had started to wonder if Johnny would have survived the wreck if he'd been better trained. Sometimes, Dylan wondered that himself.

"No," he said. He didn't want the responsibility of coaching another athlete who wouldn't listen to reason.

Letting out a shaky breath that rattled over the phone lines, Dolly said, "I was afraid of that."

"Why?"

"I needed someone of your caliber to coach one of the athletes I represent."

"I think you got the wrong guy in mind," he said, trying to wash the bitterness away with beer.

"I don't," she said. "I get it if you're not up to it. Can you recommend someone who is?"

The hell of it was, Dylan needed the money. "Are you

and your athlete all right with my track record?"

"What happened to Johnny Montana was not your fault," Dolly said.

He didn't believe her, but he appreciated that she said so.

"You made him a better rider. You couldn't have predicted what that bull did, any more than Johnny did. It was an unfortunate accident. And it terrifies me that this could happen to my…my athlete. But if you're coaching, I'll be able to sleep at night."

Dylan knew he didn't deserve that kind of trust, but he would do his damnedest to make sure that Dolly Keller kept her faith in him. "Where and when?" Dylan sighed in resignation.

"You'll do it?" Her voice lifted in excitement. "Let me check the schedule." There was a short pause. "Amarillo, Fort Worth, and San Antonio to start. Maybe the rest of the Texas circuit and Oklahoma. Then if you're a fit, the rest of the whole damned season."

Dylan closed his eyes for a second, not sure whether to be thankful for the quick three thousand dollars or to be wary because this training gig matched his schedule perfectly.

"I might not have access to the bulls at all of them." His uncle supplied bulls for some of the rodeo events and would let him use them for practice in return for some ranch hand work in the off-season. "But I can make do with a mechanical bull or hell, even rig up an oil drum if I have to. How green is the rider?"

"She's been training with Trent Campbell, so not a

complete novice."

"Hold the phone. She?" *Why on earth was a girl looking to learn how to ride a bull?*

"Yes. My sister."

Oh no.

"LeAnn."

That figured. Killer Keller would be ballsy enough to do it. He blew out a sigh. "Bull riding isn't like riding a bronc."

"I'm aware of that, and so is she. Does this change your mind?"

Dolly sounded worried, and she had a right to be. It almost made him change his mind. He didn't want to watch LeAnn ride a bull, not to mention actually training her how to do it. But he knew that LeAnn was going to do it whether or not he was the one coaching her.

What if something happened to her, like it had happened to Johnny? He forced down that thought before it could worm its way inside of him. Dylan would have to make damned sure nothing happened, that was all.

"No," he said. "I'll do it. She needs to sign a waiver, but if she wants to learn to ride, I can teach her."

"Like I said, she's ridden before. I saw her go eight seconds on a bull named Apis at Trent's school."

"I'm unfamiliar with Apis." Dylan was impressed despite himself. Trent Campbell had a good school. And if he was letting LeAnn ride, she was probably doing well, especially if she could stay on for eight seconds.

"He was terrifying." Dolly's voice shook.

Dylan had a mental image of sexy LeAnn holding on

for dear life on a nasty bull with rage in his veins. No lie. It made him a bit queasy.

"Why is she doing this?"

"Well, you didn't hear it from me—" Dolly lowered her voice "—but the WPRC is going to open up a new event for bull riding, and LeAnn wants to get a leg up on the competition."

That figured. It sounded like something the little spitfire would do. Too bad she'd been avoiding him since that night they'd slept together. He might have been able to talk her out of it. Riding broncs was one thing. Bulls were a whole other story.

"Keep it under your hat, though. Will you?"

"Not a problem." The last thing he wanted to do was listen to a bunch of cowboys bitch about women in the rodeo. The MPRC and the WPRC occasionally did joint rodeos together, but for the most part, they alternated weeks in various areas. Amarillo, Fort Worth, and San Antonio were the season openers, and both the men and women would be competing on the same weekend.

"One other thing?"

"Just one?" he drawled. He hated this. Hated that someone he cared about was willingly putting themselves at risk. But he wasn't a hypocrite. He got on a bull every damned day of his life. If he was willing to face death on four legs, he couldn't begrudge anyone else that choice. Still, it was LeAnn. Sweet, beautiful LeAnn.

"No one can know about this," Dolly continued. "LeAnn doesn't want our parents to find out until WPRC makes the announcement, so until then, it's got to be kept on the down low."

"Sure," he said, amused despite himself. Sounded like LeAnn was still tiptoeing around her family, but doing whatever she damned well wanted anyway.

"I'll wire the money in the morning, if you send me your bank information and the waiver for her to sign."

"Will do."

There was a long pause, and Dylan wondered if Dolly had hung up. But then she said, "I don't want my baby sister to get hurt."

That made two of them.

"It's a dangerous sport," he said, flashing back to that terrible moment that still haunted his every waking minute, even a year later. But he couldn't stop the memory of the last bull-riding event. And for a moment, the roaring in his head became the crowd that day. He could smell the dust and the blood, could see Johnny lying there, his neck at an unnatural angle. Dylan had to swallow a bitter rise in the back of his throat. He washed away the grief and guilt with the second beer the bartender had brought over.

"Can you keep her safe?" Dolly asked.

No. But it wouldn't be for lack of trying.

"I'll do my best to give her the skills she needs, but the rest is up to her and the bull she pulls." He reached for something comforting to say. "I can't imagine they're going to start a new event without taking a careful look at the bulls. They'll save the wild ones for the men's events." Dylan pushed the image of Johnny out of his mind.

"Right," Dolly said, and he heard her take a shaky breath. "If you don't mind, I'm going to give LeAnn your number. She'll call you when we get to Amarillo and you two can make arrangements to train."

"I'll look forward to her call." For more than a few reasons.

"Thanks." Dolly hung up after saying goodbye.

Dylan wasn't looking to get laid anymore. Not unless LeAnn was here. He had managed to put that night out of his mind when it was obvious that she wanted nothing more to do with him the next day. He figured it was because she had regrets about throwing away her virginity on the likes of him, but he hoped he hadn't scared or hurt her. It had been an intense and pleasurable few hours. She had been on top for most of it and having the time of her life. They both had been. He wished he knew what had made her avoid him for the rest of the season. Dylan chalked it up to her coming to her senses.

Across the bar room, Mick laughed in that hyena way he had, and Dylan's eyes narrowed on him. LeAnn had dated that asshole. In fact, she'd defended his bullshit right up until she caught him cheating. And Dylan had been the first man that she had seen after she had stormed out of Mick's trailer with something to prove.

A gentleman wouldn't have let her rebound into his arms.

Dylan hadn't been a gentleman. And LeAnn hadn't been interested in cooling down and taking things slow. She had been a force of nature, totally destroying the "Ice Princess" moniker that Mick had given her. She was Killer Keller in bed and Dylan had loved seeing the ruthlessness she showed in the arena when she took her pleasure with him. Shifting uncomfortably in his seat, Dylan pushed those thoughts out of his mind. She had been on fire, and he would gladly burn again.

Dylan was glad Mick hadn't managed to talk his way into LeAnn's pants. The asshat hadn't deserved her. Dylan was also pretty sure he didn't deserve LeAnn either, but at least he respected her. Mick would have taken an ad out in the rodeo bulletin if he had claimed the Ice Princess's virginity.

"What are you looking at, Porter?" Mick sneered.

"Not much," Dylan responded. "A bad bull rider with a small mind and a disgusting sense of personal hygiene."

It took a minute for Mick to process the words and realize he had been insulted. Dylan's even tone must have thrown him off his game.

"Come here and say that."

"Go outside and say it," the bartender said.

Dylan nodded. He didn't want to be banned from this place. They'd be coming back here in a few months.

"After my beer, I'll kick your ass if you still want me to," Dylan said, taking a large swallow. "And I really hope you do."

"I ain't waiting." Mick launched himself across the room at Dylan. He charged like a bull, head down, with tunnel vision. Like a bullfighter, Dylan sidestepped and Mick crashed into the barstool.

Bouncing Mick's head off the bar once for good measure, Dylan grabbed him by the back of the shirt and dragged him outside, then tossed him in the dirt of the parking lot.

"You almost made me spill my beer," Dylan said, finishing the last of it while Mick staggered to his feet. Tossing the bottle into the recycling can, he barely avoided Mick's fist. He managed to get his arm up and Mick nailed him there, instead of in his face.

So, it was like that, then. Okay.

Dylan swung with his other arm and felt Mick's nose crunch under the force of his punch. Staggering back, Mick shook his head, splattering a few drops of blood. The pain in Dylan's knuckles eased the ache in his conscience that remembering Johnny's death had caused. It felt good to get lost in a scrap, a mindless exchange of punches. Unfortunately, Mick couldn't even do that right. It was over just before it had really begun. Mick tapped out on the ground, struggling to catch his breath after Dylan's follow-up punch dropped him.

Now what?

Dylan didn't feel like going back into the bar in case Mick got his balls back along with his wind. And Dylan didn't want to risk being pulled over after having two beers, so that left him taking a walk until he was reasonably sure he'd be able to pass a Breathalyzer test.

Normally, that wouldn't be a problem—if they had been on the circuit. But it was pre-rodeo season and the only thing the MPRC had them doing was small-town shows to drum up interest for the new season. He was in a one-horse town, and the horse had gone to bed an hour ago.

His own horse, Lola, was in the barn for the night. He had given her some anti-inflammatories with the joint support medication that the last vet provided. Dylan hoped that she was resting peacefully and without pain. She had a long ride in the trailer tomorrow.

It was getting time for her to retire. Unfortunately, he didn't have a place for her to spend out her days. Not yet, anyways. He'd be damned if he would send her to his uncle's farm to be ignored. And he couldn't afford to board her while he was on the road. Not unless there were more training jobs lined up, and he won a lot this season.

As Dylan walked down the rows of closed shops, the quiet of the night started to get on his nerves. He decided to head back to the barn and check on Lola. It would give him time to sober up and then he could walk back to his truck and take it to the cheap motel he had splurged on. The small town they were in reminded him of where he grew up, and the memories soured his stomach. Maybe he should have just kept drinking to keep the ghosts of his past at bay, or maybe he should make it a point not to drink after a long day in the saddle. Either way, Dylan couldn't help but hear his uncle Lou's voice in his head.

"Don't be lazy, boy. You need to work from sunup to sundown, just to earn your keep."

Dylan had been an average teenager, and had probably been a bottomless pit when it came to his aunt's fried chicken and spareribs. Who could blame him? But he'd more than earned his keep on his uncle's ranch where his parents shuffled him off to during the summer and school vacations.

After his older brother died in a car crash, they hadn't seemed to care much about anything anymore. Danny had wrapped his car around a tree after taking a corner too fast on his sixteenth birthday. Dylan had been ten. After the accident, his parents shut down. They couldn't handle Dylan's grief on top of their own. So they sent him away.

His uncle, at least, had been more than happy to have him at the ranch, but that was because he was one less farmhand his uncle had to pay. He stayed there for a few months until school started, but nothing was ever the same again back home. Dylan was caught between wanting his old life back, with Danny taking all the risks and getting all the glory—and all of the heat from his parents—and becoming a cowboy.

"You can learn a trade," his father had said, after washing his hands of Dylan when it turned out Dylan was destined to be a straight "C" student.

"It's good for a boy to get some fresh air," his mother had said, while packing his bags.

And that was how Dylan had come to live with his aunt and uncle.

Aunt Stella had tried to make him feel at home and comfortable, but there wasn't room in the farmhouse for him, so he slept with the ranch hands, ate with the ranch hands, and worked with the ranch hands from age twelve until sixteen.

She had her hands full doing the work of three people anyway, because his uncle was too cheap to hire help. Not only did Aunt Stella cook for all of them and clean the house, but she was also in charge of the vegetable gardens, the chickens, and the egg stand down the road that sold their fresh eggs to anyone passing by.

Dylan was no stranger to hard work or ranch work, but when it turned out he had an affinity for bull riding, he started following the rodeos instead of working his uncle's farm. At sixteen, he had taken a horse his uncle had planned on sending across the border for slaughter and ran away with the rodeo.

During that season, Dylan had won enough roping events to buy an old horse trailer and a used beater of a pickup truck. His uncle had been furious, and things had been slightly strained between them ever since. If living his own life made him an ungrateful nephew, so be it. Truthfully, Dylan would've ridden a dragon if it meant he could travel from rodeo to rodeo and live out under the stars. However, after almost ten years, it had gotten old and he was ready to settle down on a ranch where he could take care of the animals that had outlived their usefulness, according to some people.

He couldn't understand why LeAnn Keller kept pushing herself. What did she have to prove? She had family who loved and supported her, and if they were a little much, at least they were there for her. She was a Texas rodeo queen and even won a few beauty pageants, if you could believe the scuttlebutt. He was curious why the perfect girl with the perfect life wanted to put her body in harm's way by riding animals that outweighed her a good ten times over, beasts that could break her in half if they hit her wrong. She was already the bronc champ. Just like she had said she was going to be.

Dylan wasn't one of those guys who thought women should only be barrel racers, but he had never trained a woman in bull riding. Hadn't trained a woman in anything, really. He hoped she didn't turn into a spoiled brat or dainty princess, because he didn't know how to handle that shit. He wasn't going to go easy on her just because she was a girl.

But he couldn't lose another athlete. He couldn't lose LeAnn.

Stopping in his tracks, Dylan looked up at the sky. Should he treat her with kid gloves? How seriously should he train her? Would he train her like he had trained Johnny? Or should he try to talk her out of riding a bull? He was worried that she was going to get injured on his watch. And if that made him a chauvinist, so be it. But his wrist was three times the size of hers, and they both gripped the same rope when they were on a bull. One wrong twist wouldn't snap his wrist like a twig, but it just might break hers. Why was she putting herself and her career at risk?

"That's none of your business," he told himself.

His job was to train her, not to give unwanted advice. Dylan probably would anyway because he couldn't help himself. Still, he hadn't convinced Johnny to stop taking risks. And he probably wouldn't stop LeAnn.

When he watched her, he could see that she loved the rodeo life. Dylan knew he wouldn't be able to stop her from riding a bull if she set her mind to it, any more than he could have stopped Johnny. But Johnny had died and Dylan had to wonder if that had been because he, as his trainer, had missed something. He should have told Johnny not to ride that crazy bull. But would it have changed anything? If Dylan was being truthful himself, he could admit that it probably wouldn't have. In fact, it might've made Johnny even more eager to get on Bulldozer.

Could he protect LeAnn from herself? Or was Dylan destined to watch another talented athlete die trying to go eight seconds and win a boatload of money?

Chapter Five

LEANN GOT A text from Dylan on the way to Amarillo. She was riding shotgun, staring out the window, trying not to be nervous about seeing him again, while Reba drove the Winnebago. Dolly was following in the pickup truck behind them, pulling Garth's trailer.

When are you arriving in Amarillo?

Even though she had had been expecting him to contact her, it still gave her a jolt. When Dolly gave her his number, LeAnn had resisted the urge to call him. What was she going to say to him? What if he brought up that night? What if he wanted her to sleep with him again?

LeAnn was more aroused than alarmed by that notion and she knew that was trouble with a capital T. It was going to be hard enough keeping the bull-riding training a secret. There would be no way she'd be able to keep the fact she was sleeping with Dylan under wraps, too.

First, her family would want to meet him. Probably over dinner. And then they'd spend the entire night embarrassing her and putting Dylan on the spot. Nope. Not going to happen. They had done that to Mick, and he nearly broke up with her because of it. She didn't need that type of aggravation in her life again. Maybe after she won the gold buckle, she'd introduce her parents to Dylan.

Maybe.

LeAnn had assigned a picture she had taken of Dylan to his phone number. It had been after he had gone eight seconds on the top bull named Implosion. Dylan was grinning wildly, his eyes full of fierce joy. LeAnn loved that picture, not only because he looked so handsome and free, but also because it perfectly portrayed how she felt after pulling off a successful ride.

She had always thought they had a lot in common. That was probably why it had been so easy for her to go to bed with him.

Leaning over to check the GPS, she saw that they were expected to arrive at the trailer park by noon. She relayed that back to Dylan. It felt strange not to start off with small talk, but then again, talking had never been their strong suit.

When do you want me?

Even though LeAnn knew he meant to meet up for training, her heart raced a little faster at the thought of being alone with him again. She hadn't been able to face him for the rest of last season. Luckily their paths hadn't crossed that often. After she pretty much used him like a sex doll the night she'd caught Mick in bed with a buckle bunny, LeAnn had been mortified by her brazenness. Dylan hadn't deserved to be treated like that. So, it was better that she stayed out of his way.

She smiled at her former naivete. It had been such a big deal for her to wait for the right man. Deep down, she had probably known that Mick wasn't the one. Dylan might not have been Mr. Right, but she was glad that she gave her virginity to someone who made her feel like she was a sex goddess.

Mick had never come close to making her shake apart with desire. If Mick's kisses had left her breathless and wanting more, she probably would've slept with him instead of coming up with excuse after excuse.

She supposed she couldn't blame Mick for getting sick of waiting for her. He hadn't made it a secret that he wanted to get laid. But Mick had lied to her and said that he was willing to wait until she was ready, that she was worth it. It turned out he was only willing to wait for her because he was seeing plenty of action on the side.

After she had lost her shit with Mick, he'd called her an untouchable little prude who needed to grow up. LeAnn wished his callous words hadn't hurt so much, and maybe that was why, when she saw Dylan in the bar, she decided to prove she wasn't a prude. Remembering her scandalous behavior still caused her to blush, but what was worse was she wanted to do it again.

I have to help my sisters set up camp first, LeAnn typed back. She cringed a little at her words. She sounded like a kid. Then again, it was no surprise to anyone that she traveled with her family. Mick would always whine, "Why do you have to spend so much time with them?"

He hadn't understood that this was a family business, that she couldn't go off like a diva and leave the chores for her sisters to do when all she did was smile for the crowds and ride. Her parents would never stand for that sort of behavior. And honestly, neither would she.

Mick had also liked to point out that they were both rodeo stars who deserved special treatment. His own parents had paid for his horses, the boarding, and all of the fees—from the comfort of their own home. She'd always been a little jealous of that. But even though her parents had been strict and occasionally unfair, unrealistic and overbearing, she knew they'd always had her best interests at heart.

Do you want to get an early dinner?

LeAnn didn't think she could face dinner with Dylan yet. That sounded too much like a date.

Sorry. I have a photo shoot and I'm not sure when I'll be free, LeAnn texted back.

Had Mick always been miserable? Had he ever really loved her? At this point, she wondered if Mick had even liked her. The worst part of it was Mick hadn't wanted to break up with her. He had just wanted to see other people because it "got lonely in other cities" when she wasn't there with him.

What Mick hadn't known was that LeAnn had been lonely even when they were in the same city together. She knew that she wasn't the most exciting girl on the rodeo circuit. And she'd never tried to be. She left that for Merry and June Grayson. Even though they'd both retired from competing, LeAnn had no real desire to take up the "Wild" mantle or June Grayson's "Bad Reputation" Stetson.

Mick had been pretty loud in voicing that having a girlfriend who traveled with most of her family put a cramp in their relationship. LeAnn had thought that they could have moved past that, except Mick had wanted to go out every night after the rodeo. That had been fun and exciting at first. But after a while, it got a little boring.

She loved to dance and play pool—everyone always underestimated her pool skills. And LeAnn wasn't above sharking a game for free drinks every now and then. But seven nights a week of drinking, partying, and telling the same old stories to different fans in different cities became tedious. And worse, it had affected her performance in the arena.

It would have been nice to do something different for a change. A nice steak dinner would have been a change of pace. Going out to a movie or having an ice cream while taking a walk exploring some of the cities they were in would have gone a long way to easing her loneliness. After all, after doing five cities in five weeks, the inside of the bars all started to look alike.

As she always did when she thought of Mick, LeAnn compared him to Dylan. But honestly, there was no comparison. Mick was still a boy—a spoiled little boy. Dylan was very much a man.

Still, as much as she was attracted to Dylan, she had to stay focused on the season. LeAnn had to have her priorities straight. This was her go-big or go-home moment, and she couldn't throw that all away on some guy with bedroom eyes and a mouth made for kissing.

Do you want to practice tonight, or not?

LeAnn made a face. She had a feeling that she had pissed him off. *Yes. Is seven p.m. too late?* she texted.

Fine. Meet me outside of barn A.

And it was done. LeAnn blew out a long sigh. She had

hoped that Dylan hadn't taken this job thinking that she was going to fall into his bed. She hoped that he would treat her as seriously as he would a man who was coming to him for training. LeAnn didn't know what she would do if Dylan turned out to be a condescending jerk about this.

A part of her hoped he had dismissed their reckless night of passion. After all, it was more common for the guys to have wild flings, right? The other part of her would be mortally offended if he didn't think it had been special. It had been wild and wonderful, and she knew that she hadn't been alone in being blown away by that night. She didn't know what she wanted. That was how crazy he made her. Except, she couldn't deny that she wanted to see him again.

She should have dated Dylan instead of Mick. LeAnn couldn't help thinking about how things would have been different if she had hooked up with him all those years ago.

LEANN COULDN'T WAIT for the photo shoot to be over. Her face hurt from smiling, her head was throbbing, and her leg was falling asleep. The WPRC had a huge social media blitz planned and they needed lots of pictures to populate it.

"Remember to look in the camera and smile," Dolly said from the sidelines.

While LeAnn was glad she had somebody like Dolly helping her out with the public relations stuff, she hated being micromanaged. Stand here. Look there. LeAnn just wanted to ride a bull. She didn't understand why all of this was necessary when the WPRC hadn't even announced the new bull-riding event yet. But then again, she didn't have to. That was Dolly's job, and she was damned good at it. So if Dolly said look at the camera and smile, even though that advice seemed obvious and a little annoying after a long day of traveling, LeAnn would do what her sister asked.

"Okay, visualize your success. Portray the woman you want to be."

Except when she said woo-woo shit like that. The problem was, LeAnn didn't know who she was. She started out as a beauty pageant queen as a teenager who segued into WPRC's "America's sweetheart." Then she turned eighteen and put a black mark on her reputation by drinking and mooning a cop. She lost her parents' trust, her sponsors and the bronc belt and title. After three years of fighting and scratching her way back, she was a decent barrel racer, a damned good bronc buster, and maybe a contender for the bull-riding buckle. She had five months, five states and twenty events to make it happen if the WPRC announced the new event tomorrow.

"You call that a smile?" Dolly said. "It looks like you're grimacing."

"How about now?" LeAnn crossed her eyes and stuck out her tongue.

Dolly gave her an exasperated look. "If you're not going to be serious about this, we're going to take pictures of Garth instead."

"He's probably more photogenic right now," LeAnn

said, rubbing her temples.

Frowning in concern, Dolly said, "Okay, we're done here."

"Thanks," LeAnn said, knowing that her sister saw the warning signs. She had a migraine that felt like her worst hangover. And since she had given up partying after making one bad mistake after another—one of them being Mick—that was saying something.

Sometimes the whole rodeo scene left her wanting more. But more of what, she wasn't sure. All LeAnn knew was that when she thought of life after rodeo, she didn't see anything but a great big maw of nothing. Riding horses was her life. She was going to add bulls to that too, and hopefully a picture of what life after rodeo would look like would come to her.

When the photographer had left, LeAnn went up to her sister and spoke in a low voice. "Any word on the announcement?"

Dolly shook her head. "Not a peep."

"They're still going through with it though, right?" LeAnn hoped they weren't going to put it off until next season. Although, it would give her more time to practice.

"Of course. They need to get attendance up. Don't worry, they're probably just planning something big." Bolstered by the success of the women's bronc-busting category, the WPRC was eager to get more butts in the seats. And that meant thinking out of the box, or in this case, the rodeo arena with these photo shoots.

Dolly went off to find more reliable internet, so Reba helped her get Garth back into the horse trailer.

"Do you want me to take a ride to the barn with you?" Reba asked.

"No thanks, I got this. I'll probably stay late and catch up with some friends." LeAnn wondered if Dolly had told her about the bull-riding lessons.

Reba bit her lip. "Maybe I should go."

"I'll be fine." LeAnn laid her hand on her sister's arm. "I just need some me time."

Nodding, Reba grinned. "I hear that. I'm looking forward to just relaxing tonight too. But call if you need me, or if Garth is having a problem settling in."

"Will do," LeAnn said, glad that Reba hadn't pushed the issue about chaperoning her. Her sisters, at least, were starting to realize that LeAnn wouldn't fall into catastrophe if she was left alone for a few hours. Being the baby of the family wasn't easy, even when you didn't royally screw up.

LeAnn drove the pickup truck to the rodeo arena, pulling into the lot where all the other horse trailers were. Garth was used to the routine, and she was able to get him out of the trailer without any assistance. She saddled him up and took him for a couple laps around the arena at a slow pace to warm up. Then when he was ready, she waited her turn to practice doing a clover leaf around the barrels with him. LeAnn could tell that he was happy for the exercise. So was she.

This year LeAnn was going to compete in all the events. She wanted to keep her competitive edge sharp. And on the off chance that the WPRC wasn't going to introduce bull riding this year, LeAnn could use the exposure of winning other events to attract more sponsors.

After confirming with the rodeo staff where she needed to stable Garth, LeAnn went over the information for tomorrow's event. She was honored to see that the WPRC wanted her and Garth to carry out the Texas flag during the opening ceremonies.

LeAnn wondered if that was Dolly's doing, because they hadn't asked her to do that ever since she had lost to Merry. And as if her thoughts had conjured her up, Merry Grayson was standing right behind her when she turned around.

"Hiya, Killer," Merry said. She had a toddler perched on her hip, but other than that, she looked the same, if a little bit tired.

"You're not competing this year, are you?" For one horrified moment, LeAnn wondered if Merry had come out of retirement to try for the bull-riding buckle.

"Oh hell no. I'm announcing."

LeAnn tried to keep the relief off her face, but Merry must have seen it anyway because she laughed.

"I'm not even getting on a horse. But I think June will be doing some pickup riding during the season."

"How have you been?" LeAnn asked, smiling at the toddler who was alternating peeking at her and burying her face in her mother's shirt.

"Busy, but I'm looking forward to traveling a bit on the circuit again. I've missed it. Not enough to get back on a horse, but there's something about the rodeo, you know?" Merry smiled wistfully.

"I do."

"Let's have a girls' night and go out for drinks soon.

Simon over there can watch Kaila and we can kick it up." She pointed out at a handsome man who was leaning against a purple Corvette.

"Daddy!" the toddler cried, squirming.

Merry set her down and the little girl took off running toward her father.

"I'd like that," LeAnn said. Maybe Merry could give her some advice on how to attract a big sponsor or maybe even put in a good word for her.

"Here's my phone number." Merry texted it to her. "Good luck tomorrow."

"Thanks." LeAnn watched as she joined her family and felt a pang of something she couldn't identify. It looked like there was life after rodeo after all, and it kind of looked nice.

Chapter Six

DYLAN WAS NERVOUS about seeing LeAnn again, which was ridiculous. He just had to treat her like any other student. Of course, she was the only student he'd ever slept with. He got to the barn a few minutes early because he didn't want to keep her waiting. There were still some stragglers around and he wondered if that was going to be a problem for LeAnn's need for secrecy.

He decided to check on Lola while he waited for LeAnn to show up. His horse was doing fine, and he stroked her nose affectionately. She had a few more rides left in her. So did he, but he was aware that the clock was ticking for his bull-riding career as well. It was just a matter of time before he landed wrong or a bull got in a good shot.

"Oh, you're here," LeAnn said, popping up from inside her horse's stall down the same row Lola was in.

"What are you doing in there?" he asked, frowning at how stiff she was moving.

"Nothing. No reason. Look, let's just get started."

Dylan paused, wondering if he should mention the elephant in the room. But her eyes darted everywhere but to him and he didn't want to make her nervous. If she wanted to pretend that nothing had happened, he was okay with that. Reaching out to her, he helped her out of the stall. She looked good, if a little rumpled. Her blond hair was pulled back into a ponytail, but a few wispy strands escaped it to frame her heart-shaped face.

"You've got straw in your hair," he said, carefully plucking it out.

Her eyes wide, she just stared at him. Even with dirt smudged on her face, LeAnn still looked cute as hell. It was hard to resist the urge to kiss the tip of her upturned nose before claiming her full luscious mouth. One kiss was all he wanted. One kiss to remember how sweet it was, and to assure himself that the passion that had exploded between them that night was just the circumstances and not the norm.

Dylan let his fingers linger and trail down her cheek. He tipped up her chin, planning on just a quick kiss. LeAnn continued to watch him, mesmerized. He gave her plenty of time to stop him as he leaned down to kiss her. When she put her hand on his shoulder, though, it wasn't to push him away, but to softly move it up to the back of his neck. That was all the encouragement he needed. He brushed a kiss on her forehead, then to the tip of her nose, and then finally Dylan gave in and crushed his mouth on hers.

Her mouth was as sweet as he remembered. She kissed him back eagerly, pressing closer against him. He hugged her to him tightly, reaching down to cup her ass as he deepened the kiss. Dylan wasn't sure how long they spent kissing. But he knew he needed to breathe or he was going to pass out. Lifting his head, he managed to whisper,

"Well, hello, LeAnn. Why have you been avoiding me?"

She blinked at him as if coming back to her senses. Taking a deep breath, LeAnn pushed him away. He took a step back to give them both some room. His head was still fuzzy and reeling from her kisses. A part of him wanted to say to hell with the training lessons. He wanted to take her back to his hotel room and see where this passion led them.

"I treated you poorly that night," she said, looking down at her hands. "And I'm sorry for that."

Poorly? Dylan barked out a laugh. "Sweetheart, if that was poor, I don't think I could have survived you treating me well."

LeAnn crossed her arms and gave him a glare that would've been scary on a six-foot-five man, but it only made LeAnn look like an enraged kitten. He knew better than to tell her that, though.

"You know what I meant. I used you for sex and I ordered you around like a drill sergeant."

"I was strangely all right with that."

She looked less angry, but she still rolled her eyes at him. "I know that. It's because you're a guy. But I don't do things like that."

"I know. I was there. I was your first."

She blushed a fiery crimson, but she didn't back down. "Yes, I know. I was there too. I chose you."

"I'm honored," Dylan said. "And I mean that."

"I know I'm not like a lot of women you're used to being with. I'm not a buckle bunny. I'm a lot more inexperienced. And aside from that one crazy night, I equate sex with love, and I know that most people don't."

Fair enough. Before he could say anything, LeAnn continued.

"I was waiting until I fell in love with someone before I had sex with them. I thought I was ready to be with Mick, but something kept stopping me from going through with it."

"Common sense?" Dylan drawled.

She smiled, but it seemed forced. "Must have been. Or divine intervention. I don't know. Then it didn't seem to matter anymore. I wanted to hurt Mick. I wanted to have a revenge fling." She looked up at him with sorrow in her eyes. "So I used you."

"That's all right," he said, feeling a little hurt even though he didn't know why.

"Do you want a girlfriend?"

Did he? What could he offer a girlfriend? He didn't even book a motel room tonight and had planned on warming something up in his hotpot that plugged into his truck's twelve-volt power outlet.

She laughed. "You should see the look on your face."

"I'm sorry, you just caught me off guard."

"I was messing with you." LeAnn relaxed more and her smile was more natural. "I had fun that night."

"I did too."

"I don't want to pretend it never happened," she said. "But I'm not the type of girl who will ever be into casual sex."

"It's okay," Dylan said.

"No matter how tempted I am."

Pleasure flared through him. "Are you tempted?"

She nodded, but held out a hand to stop him from moving closer. "I'm not making ultimatums here. I'm just telling it like it is. The next time I have sex, it's going to be with a man I'm in a committed relationship with. If that can't be you, then move along."

"I hear you," he said. He could be monogamous. That was easy. It was the other expectations that came with being in a relationship that made him wary of commitment. He called his truck his home. He was never in one place for more than a week because he followed the rodeos all over the United States, and when he could afford it, he went down to Mexico and South America in the off-season to compete down there.

"Is it going to be difficult to work with me as your trainer?" he asked, wanting to hold her against him. She looked like she needed a hug after saying all of that to him. Or maybe he needed one. Which was ridiculous because he had never needed a hug in his whole damned life.

"It might get weird, but I can handle it if you can." She lifted her chin defiantly up at him.

Challenge accepted.

"All right then," he said. "Let's get started. We've got a couple of choices. There's a bull-riding machine set up by the games of chance. The ride operator is a buddy of mine and he'll let me run the controls. Or we can go to a park that I know of that has some oil drums set up and I can pull the lever and see what you've got."

"What about a real bull?" LeAnn asked, putting her hands on her hips. "I can ride a real bull."

"Not without a crew you can't. I need to arrange a gate

man and some bullfighters. You're also going to have to practice with the men. There's no keeping this a secret once you start doing that. Cowboys gossip like little old ladies. It'll get back to your parents."

LeAnn nibbled on her lower lip while she thought about it. He hoped she wouldn't insist on the bulls. Some of them were regular sons of bitches. He'd have to snoop around and see if there was a milder bull in the bunch that one of the owners would let them use for practice so it could get experience along with LeAnn.

"Set it up," she finally said. "I'll do the mechanical tonight. But I want to get practice in on a live animal from now on. Once the WPRC makes their announcement, anyway, there won't be any need to keep this a secret."

"Okay," he said. Dylan didn't like it, but she was the boss.

Stretching, LeAnn grimaced and rubbed the center of her back.

"Are you all right?" Dylan asked.

"Yeah, just a little stiff from the long drive and from sitting in my horse stall for about an hour."

Dylan's eyes narrowed on her horse. "Is something wrong with him?"

"No, he's fine. I was hunkered down there to avoid people I didn't want to talk to. It was a little cramped."

"Who were you avoiding?"

"Mick." She grimaced. "I know that makes me a coward, but I can't deal with him right now. Let's just get started, okay?"

Dylan let it drop because it was obvious that she wanted to change the subject, but if Mick was making a pest of himself, Dylan would take care of it.

They made their way over to the midway section of the rodeo. Vendors were setting up tents of merchandise to beat the rush when the rodeo opened tomorrow morning. There was almost a carnival-like feel in the air. In the center of the games and attractions, there was a mechanical bull surrounded by thick mats and a realistic-looking fence.

"Wait here," Dylan said, going up to one of the guys he recognized. The man was fiddling with an electronic panel.

"Okay." LeAnn shrugged and wandered over to a table with a stack of leather pocketbooks on it.

"Hey, Chris," Dylan said. "How's it going?"

"Mary Kate is on my case again. She says I don't spend enough time with her. Can you blame me? All she does is nag, nag, nag."

Dylan smirked. "What's she nagging you about?"

"That all I do is sit around the house and do nothing when there are things that need to get fixed—that sort of thing. How about you?"

"I'm trying to show my friend over there a good time." Dylan inclined his head in LeAnn's direction.

"Holy shit, is that the Killer?" Chris asked.

"Yeah, it sure is. I bet her that she can't go eight seconds on this mechanical bull. As you can imagine, she doesn't want to do it in front of an audience. So, we were hoping to do that tonight while there's not a lot of people around. Can you make that possible?"

"Say no more," Chris said. "It is just about time for my coffee break anyway. Do you remember how to run the machine?"

Dylan nodded. "I remember. Here's twenty bucks for your time." It was his last twenty, until LeAnn's tuition money cleared the bank, but that was okay. He'd make it work. He always did.

Chris put his hands in his pockets. "You don't have to do that. I still owe you for all those times you covered for me when I was having a smoke break or taking Mary Kate on the rides."

"Nah, you paid me in hot dogs and lemonade for doing that. Most of the time, that was the only meal I had back then. We're even. Keep the twenty," Dylan said. "Use it to take care of some of the chores Mary Kate is complaining about."

Chris gave him a considering look and accepted the bill. "I like how you think. Have fun."

When he was gone, Dylan beckoned LeAnn over. "Okay, let's see what you can do."

No lie, it was a joy to watch her crawl up on the mechanical bull. He had a couple of uncomfortable moments when he pictured her jumping on top of him and wiggling around like that. But by the time she'd settled on top, Dylan was all business. Once she was in position and gripping the rope, she gave him a nod. He started the bull off slow.

"Give me a break," LeAnn said as the bull made a languorous turn and bumped up and down in slow motion.

"I'm getting a look at your form. It's good." He wasn't being a pervert when he said that, but that form was excellent as well. She held herself like a bull rider and was balanced and steady.

"I'm going to increase the speed slowly."

"Yeah," she said sarcastically. "Because that's how it happens in real life."

Dylan was tempted to jam the machine up to ten so it tossed her on her ass, but this wasn't a pissing match. He was getting paid to teach her how to ride a bull. But it didn't matter how much money he was being paid. If he didn't like what he saw, there was no way Dylan was going to put her on a real bull.

LeAnn handled herself well and when she started to look bored, Dylan increased the speed. Her body moved to compensate for the jerking movements of the bull. When he turned the dial and adjusted the controls to a level a professional bull rider would practice on, she held her own for a little over eight seconds. She eventually spun off and landed on her feet, though the mats pushed her off-balance a little bit, and she staggered.

"That feels a lot better than hitting the arena floor," she said.

"Okay," he said. "I've seen enough."

She put her hands on her hips. "What do you mean? What did I do wrong?"

"You didn't do anything wrong. Get back on the bull. And this time, I'm setting the level at max."

Shock warred with pure joy and excitement on her face, and Dylan couldn't help returning the grin. LeAnn understood how it felt. She was a kindred spirit. And he had a feeling she was going to give everyone in the bull-riding event a run for their money.

LeAnn clambered on the bull again and gave him the

nod. Dylan turned on the machine to max, and pressed start.

"Feet in. Chest out. Tuck your damned head. Shoulders back," Dylan barked. "When the bull twists to the left, drop your hand down a bit. That's right."

He put her through five more rides, noting the areas where she needed to improve. After she took a little longer getting up from the last one, he shut off the machine and walked out to the mats to help her up.

"That was awesome," LeAnn said, still grinning.

"You did good, Killer." He hoisted her to her feet and helped her climb off the mats.

"So next time, we're going to do this again, but with real bulls?"

He hesitated. Johnny had been eager like this. He wasn't going to make the same mistakes he had with Johnny with her. "First thing we're going to do is work on your core. You're going to hit the gym every day. I want to see you doing squats, and working with the balance board and yoga ball."

At her look of disappointment, he qualified that with, "You've got the whole rodeo season ahead of you. Before I take the risk of you getting injured on my watch, I want to make sure you're conditioned enough to handle what the bulls can throw at you day after day."

"That seems fair," she said grudgingly.

"Don't think you're getting out of cardio either."

"Ugh."

They started walking back to the barn. Dylan resisted the urge to hold her hand. "Don't worry. We'll get some bull time in. I need to find you some smaller bulls, though." And he needed to come to terms with seeing her on one. She was competent. If she had been a man, he wouldn't be feeling like this. Johnny had scarred him, though. Dylan just wanted to wrap her in Bubble Wrap and keep her safe. But he knew she'd never stand for that crap.

"I don't need special treatment. You can call Trent Campbell," she said. "He'll let you know that for the last six weeks, I've been riding bulls of all sizes."

"I appreciate the heads-up," he said. "You should give him a call and let them know it's okay to talk to me. He and I can come up with a decent training schedule based on your experience. And don't worry, you'll get your chance on the bigger bulls. I won't feel right about it though until I see how you handle the little ones."

"So, you think I did all right?" LeAnn stared at her fingernails, as if his answer wouldn't bother her. But he could tell that what he was about to say would mean a great deal to her.

"I'm going to be honest with you," he said. "As a man who knows how dangerous these creatures are, I don't like the idea of you or any other woman on a bull."

Bristling, her hands clenched into fists. Dylan knew he had to speak fast because he didn't want to lose her before he got to the important part.

"But that being said, bull riding is a dangerous sport whether you're a man or woman. Injuries happen. Death happens. But you can also die in a car crash on the highway. There are no guarantees in life. When I look at you, whether it's on a bronc or on a mechanical bull, I can see that this is your passion, and this is something that makes life worth living for you. I feel the same way about the sport. So, I get it. I get what drives you."

She looked up at him, unshed tears shining in her eyes. It made him uncomfortable, and he looked away.

"You've got good form. Trent Campbell taught you well. But I think you had the basics of it long before he started training you, and that gave you a decent start."

LeAnn nodded quickly. "I did. I started out on mechanical bulls when I could sneak on one. And that doesn't even count the homemade rigs that I went on as a kid when my parents weren't looking."

"Same," Dylan said. "So because of all that, I think you have what it takes to be a champion in this event."

LeAnn stopped in her tracks and took a shuddering breath. She laid a hand on his arm and squeezed it. "Thank you," she whispered. "You're the first person to say that."

He slung an arm around her shoulder and tugged her in for a quick hug. "I'm sorry about that. If you had been a man, you would have been getting all the encouragement you needed. You chose a hard path, but that doesn't mean it's going to be hard all the time." He wished he could stop worrying that she'd get hurt. Injuries were a part of their life. He just didn't want to see her crushed into the ground. It made him panicky to think of her like that.

"Once the WPRC makes their announcement," LeAnn said, "I think there is going to be a bit of a backlash. But after the first couple events, it'll be like the bronc busting. Just another event."

When they reached the barn, Dylan asked, "Are there any other women that you know of eager to do this event?"

"Why?" she asked, looking at him from under her lashes. "Are you looking to expand your training schedule?"

"No." He gave a short laugh. "Like I don't have enough on my hands with my own schedule and training you. I was wondering how many takers the WPRC was going to have. Part of the training will be looking at your competition."

"I appreciate you doing this for me," LeAnn said. "I haven't really talked to the other women on the circuit yet. We don't keep in touch during the off-season." She shrugged. "It's hard to get close to people when you're not on the road with them. That's one of the things I felt that I missed out on while traveling with my family."

"You haven't missed much," Dylan said. "At least you don't have to worry about coming back to your hotel room and seeing that your roommate brought a girl home. Trust me, sleeping in the bathtub while they're going at it like rabbits all night is not conducive to a good ride the next morning."

"Yeah," LeAnn said, smiling. "But I bet no one wakes you up at six o'clock in the morning singing Tammy Wynette songs while hogging the bathroom."

"No, that would be a new experience for me."

"Just once, I want to sleep late and have the bathroom all to myself."

"It's good to have goals," Dylan said.

"I should get going before my sisters come looking for me. They're overprotective."

Dylan wanted to tell her how much he enjoyed tonight.

But he didn't want to make it weird. He also wanted to kiss her good night, but he wasn't sure that the kiss would be enough for either of them. So he walked her back to her car, wishing they could prolong their conversation. As he watched her drive away, he wondered if they could make a long-distance relationship work when they were both in different states at different rodeos. Dylan knew he should concentrate on just being the best damned coach to LeAnn that he could be. But a part of him wanted a shot at being more than her coach. He just didn't want to risk being a distraction, because winning was what she wanted more than anything. He wanted that for her too. All he had to do was keep her safe while she achieved it.

Chapter Seven

DYLAN WENT BACK to the barn to check on Lola one last time. The lights were still on even though most of the crowd had gone home. He wondered who the hell was still here. He hadn't counted on having company. If he had wanted to chit-chat, he would have gone to a bar. He was surprised, however, that the two men in the barn weren't cowboys. They were suits. They weren't actually wearing suits, but their Levi's were bright blue, and crisply pressed. Their shirts were clean, unwrinkled white Oxford shirts, with real silver bolo lariats around their necks studded with shiny stones. Since they were nowhere near his horse, Dylan figured he'd just ignore them, but they looked up when he entered the barn.

"Dylan Porter, good to see you." The man with the onyx bolo tie came over to him, holding out his hand. He looked like a cross between a used car salesman and a mafia hitman. He had slicked-back hair and an easy grin that didn't reach his eyes.

Dylan had no idea who the hell this was, but he forced a smile and shook the man's hand anyway. "It's too nice of a night to be hanging out in a barn," Dylan said, hoping for some context clues on who these guys were.

"I'm just giving Mr. Hickory a tour of some of our athletes," Onyx Bolo said, patting a horse on the neck.

Mr. Hickory, whose bolo tie had what looked to be real turquoise on it, piped up, "We just came from seeing the bulls. Mean sons of bitches, aren't they?"

"Not usually," Dylan said. "Not this time of night, anyway."

"Well, that's probably because they don't have a rope around their balls like they do when they're in the chute."

Dylan didn't know who Mr. Hickory was, but it was obvious he was an idiot and knew nothing about bull riding. "The rope doesn't go around their balls. It goes around their back haunches. And that's not what causes them to kick and fuss. They're bred to do that."

"Maybe not up here, but I'm more familiar with those Mexican fighting bulls. Those sons of bitches are ornery and mean as hell."

"Yeah, they are."

"But I would be too if I had a rope around my balls."

Dylan wasn't going to argue. It wasn't as if this man was ever going to get on a bull anyway. As long as he wasn't from PETA or another animal activist group, it didn't matter. It wasn't Dylan's job to defend the rodeo circuit. He turned away to check on Lola's food and water and to murmur a few words of encouragement. He was relieved to see that Lola's eyes were no longer clouded in pain. At least one of them would be resting comfortably tonight.

"So how you feel about your chances in Fort Worth next week?" Mr. Hickory said.

"I'm going to win," Dylan said. Was there another answer to that question?

"Good. I placed a bet on you. Don't lose me money now."

"I'll try not to."

"If you want, you can give me some money and I'll put in a bet for you on your behalf. You could earn some extra cash that way."

Wasn't a bad idea. Once LeAnn's tuition cleared, he'd have a thousand dollars. It would be nice to double that.

"Now, Mr. Hickory, you know that's against the MPRC's rules," Onyx Bolo said.

Was it?

Dylan had never bothered to check the handbook they'd given him when he first started traveling the circuit. But apparently Onyx Bolo was a corporate shill.

"Jackson, don't be such a stick in the mud," Mr. Hickory said.

Dylan stiffened. Jackson? Jackson Blevins? Great. He was in the barn with the chief executive officer of the Men's Professional Rodeo Circuit of America. If that wasn't an invitation to get the hell out of here, nothing was.

With a last pat for his horse, Dylan said, "I should be going. I'll leave you to your evening, gentlemen."

"Hold on there, son," Mr. Hickory said. "Don't go running off. We were just going to get a few drinks back at the head office and talk about an opportunity for the MPRC to assist the WPRC. And I think you'd be the right person for the job."

A job? Just who the hell was Mr. Hickory?

Jackson looked Dylan up and down, frowning in

thought. Then he slowly nodded. "You might be onto something, Mr. Hickory."

Oh shit. What did he get himself into now?

"Come on," Mr. Hickory said. "My driver's just outside."

Dylan didn't have a graceful way out, and truth be told, he was a little curious about Mr. Hickory and whatever the role they saw for Dylan in the MPRC was—especially if it came with a hefty paycheck or something that would help him build a nest egg so he could put a down payment on that farm he'd been eyeing. He'd do just about anything to give Lola a break from traveling from rodeo to rodeo.

Dylan was afraid to use the "H" word yet. Home. Was he sick of sleeping in his truck or in a flop hotel when he had the money? Yeah, who wouldn't be? But it went beyond that. He wanted a place where his horse could live out her days in comfort and not be threatened to go to the glue factory or the slaughterhouse, like his uncle's horses. And if that meant he had to sit and have a drink with a couple of suits, he'd do it.

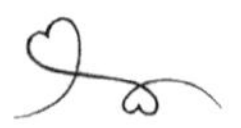

THE HOME OFFICE was a showpiece building. Large outside screens on the side of the building broadcasted the latest rodeo highlights to the busy streets below. Inside was an architectural glory of steel and glass with enough down-home country décor to make it seem like it was a legitimate Old West enterprise. Dylan had heard rumors that the company was in serious financial trouble but looking around at the building, he wondered if that was all they were, just rumors.

"First time here?" Jackson asked.

Dylan nodded.

"She's something isn't she?" Mr. Hickory said as they got into the elevator.

"Impressive," Dylan said.

The elevator ride was fast and a little disorienting, but it was nothing like riding a bull. Once the elevator doors opened up, they stepped out into a wide corridor. On the walls there were framed pictures of all of the MPRC champions from his boyhood idol Hank Teller to the more recent legend Trent Campbell.

"Someday that's going to be you on that wall," Mr. Hickory said.

"Maybe."

They turned into an opulent conference room that was stocked with a full bar. Wall-to-wall windows overlooked the busy street below.

"Beer or whiskey?" Jackson asked.

"Whiskey," Dylan replied.

"That's my boy," Mr. Hickory said and clapped him on the shoulder.

When they all had their drinks and were sitting around the table, Mr. Hickory leaned in. "I'm not going to beat around the bush."

Dylan sipped his drink. It was the good stuff, and it was free. He'd listen as long as they kept pouring.

"We saw you and Killer Keller out practicing."

Fingers tightening on his glass, Dylan wondered how

much they saw. Had they seen the kiss?

"She's a firecracker, isn't she?" Jackson said.

"She's a talented athlete," Dylan said.

"Did her sister hire you to train her?" Jackson asked.

"I'm training her," Dylan confirmed, bracing for the condemnation. Whether it was about training a woman or about taking on another student so soon after Johnny's death.

Jackson and Mr. Hickory exchanged looks. "That's good. Real good. It makes things easier," Jackson said.

"Easier how?" Their reaction confused him.

"This stays between us," Jackson said. "But the WPRC is going to announce that they're opening up a new event at the rodeo tomorrow. You must have heard the rumor. I know LeAnn Keller has."

"It's been bandied about."

"Well, during the MPRC's event tomorrow, there's going to be a woman entered in the bull-riding event with you men. She's going to go last, and it will be a surprise addition."

"Who?" If it had been LeAnn, she would have mentioned it.

"Well, we would have asked Killer if we'd known she was interested. But this might actually work out better. Have you heard of Muriel Degas?"

Crap.

"Yeah, I know Muriel." He didn't know she was a bull rider though. When they had hooked up a year or so ago, she was just doing bronc riding. He had been clear from the beginning he was only looking for a good time for one night. She had wanted more. This had the potential to get real awkward, real quick.

"She's going to give it her all, and hopefully go the full eight seconds."

"On what bull?" Tension tightened his shoulders and he felt that familiar sickness in his gut.

"One of mine," Mr. Hickory said. "I just bought a line of bull stock that I'm leasing to the WPRC. They're young, three and four years. Most have competed as yearlings. They're not as tough as the ones you boys go on, but they'd be perfect for the ladies."

"So where do I fit into all of this?" Dylan asked.

"I wanted an experienced bull rider to assess my new bulls."

"You've got an uncle in this business, don't you?" Jackson tapped on a few keys on a laptop. "Lou Porter, right?"

"Yeah, I grew up on his cattle ranch."

"I know your uncle," Mr. Hickory said. "He speaks very highly of you."

"He does?" Dylan almost choked on his whiskey. That was news to him.

"He said he taught you everything he knows, and then you left him to ride bulls instead of work on the ranch."

Now that sounded like his uncle. "I left to be a rodeo cowboy. The bulls were just for fun."

"You're familiar with your uncle's bulls, though."

Dylan nodded. "Yeah, I've ridden them in competition before."

"I knew when I saw you that you were perfect for this job I have in mind."

"A job?" Dylan wondered where this was going. "Doing what exactly?"

"Sorting the bulls, keeping your ears out for anything that could improve our profits, that sort of thing," Jackson said.

"How does sixty thousand a year sound for a salary?" Mr. Hickory asked.

It sounded pretty good. Sixty thousand on top of everything else could be a down payment on a place that Lola could retire to. He could get a new horse too. And if he had a great season, he might be able to start the rescue business up sooner rather than later. He strove to keep the elation he was feeling off his face. He didn't want to appear too eager, but he was already calculating his first paycheck and where to spend it.

"Can I still compete?" Dylan asked.

"As long as it doesn't interfere with you assessing those bulls," Mr. Hickory said.

"I can do that." It would be good to make sure that the women wouldn't be on dangerous animals. It was a win-win situation. However, it did have the potential to blow up in his face. But he figured he could handle the backlash if it became public knowledge that the women were getting milder bulls than the men.

"I don't want to put Killer on a killer, if you know what I mean," Mr. Hickory said.

Dylan nodded. They were on the same page there. But there was something that wasn't clear to him. "Why is the MPRC involved with WPRC bulls?"

"Shelby Miller, the CEO of the women's rodeo, asked

for our help. After all, we've been doing this forever and since bull riding is a new event for her, she wants to make sure her athletes are safe," Jackson said.

That was a relief.

"Besides, and this stays in this room, it might be time to combine the women's and the men's rodeo into one big company. With venues being scarce and costs on the rise, it could be a big crowd pleaser to have one large weekend show where the fans could see all their favorite riders."

It would also mean that he and LeAnn would be traveling together. Dylan liked the idea of seeing her more often and who knew? Maybe they could try a relationship? Stranger things had happened on the road.

"But that's putting the cart before the horse," Jackson said. "Right now, the ladies have their own calendar of events for this year, but you can be sure we're going to be looking at the numbers when we're at the same venue."

"Like we are tomorrow, and then again in Fort Worth and San Antonio."

"That's right," Jackson said.

Mr. Hickory refilled their glasses. "The bulls that show promise will get promoted to the men's events and eventually go out to stud. The ones that aren't so exciting will be reserved for the women's events."

That wouldn't go over well with LeAnn if it became common knowledge, but Dylan was strangely comfortable with it. "Are you sure that won't take the excitement out of the event for the audience?" he asked. Not to mention for the women athletes.

"Not necessarily. These bulls aren't pussy cats after all.

Besides, when we announce the event after Ms. Degas's wild ride, we're hoping to go viral," Jackson said. "Can you confirm that Killer is going to throw her hat in the ring and compete?"

"Yes, she definitely is." Dylan knew he should probably tell Jackson to talk with LeAnn himself, but he didn't think it would do any harm to confirm what they all already knew.

"Good. She's very photogenic. I'll advise Shelby to throw some marketing behind her. Her sister, Dolly, knows how to sling the bullshit. This will get some butts in the seats," Jackson said. "It's been a hard couple of years profit-wise for both the organizations, so we're looking to do more joint promotions to pool resources. Wasn't she dating Luke Mickleson?"

Dylan fought not to grind his teeth. "Yeah, it was an ugly breakup."

Jackson snorted. "Too bad. They look good together."

Not if Dylan messed up his pretty face. He allowed himself a small smile at the thought.

"They could be the glue that sticks the two organizations together," Mr. Hickory said.

"Mick's a piece of shit," Dylan said and then shrugged at their shocked looks. "Ask around. If you're looking for a wholesome image, he's not your guy."

"Neither is Killer. She had some issues a few years ago," Mr. Hickory said.

Dylan felt the need to defend LeAnn. "She was a kid. Who didn't make a few mistakes when they were that age?"

"True," Mr. Hickory said.

"It's all about winning," Mr. Jackson said. "That's what's keeping the fans from coming back."

"LeAnn's a winner," Dylan said confidently.

"I'm sure Shelby is keeping an eye on her."

"Aside from letting Muriel ride in tomorrow's event, how much more will the MPRCA be involved in the women's event?" Dylan asked.

"Officially, not at all."

"Really?" Dylan was surprised, because Jackson seemed to be concentrating on the women riders more than he was his own athletes. If he knew anything about the bull riders, Mick would not have been anyone's choice to represent the organization. Mick was a petulant, reckless, entitled ass—and those were his good points.

"There's been some pushback, as the women's organization is worried that they'll lose out on television and event programming, if we merge. But it makes financial sense in the long run." Jackson stared at him coldly. "I need to remind you that the potential for this acquisition is not for public knowledge."

"I don't gossip," he said.

"I'm glad to hear that," Mr. Hickory said.

"One other thing," Jackson said.

There was always a catch.

"We'd appreciate it if you would do everything in your power to make sure that LeAnn Keller wins the buckle."

"That's what she's paying me for," Dylan said. "But why do you two want her to win over Muriel or the other women?"

Easing back in his chair, Jackson took a sip of his drink.

"She's got the right look that the WPRC wants to promote, and she's got the spirit and drive that people respond to."

"And after she lost the bronc busting to Merry Grayson, the odds are against her winning the bull-riding event. A cagey better could take home serious dividends," Mr. Hickory said.

"You're going to bet on LeAnn?" Dylan said.

"It's smart money," Mr. Hickory said with a look at Jackson.

"It's a conflict of interest," Jackson said, and shot Dylan a warning look. "Our athletes don't bet on each other."

"But I'm not an athlete," Mr. Hickory said amiably. "What do you say, boy? Do you think you can help us pick out winning bulls?"

His uncle was going to have a few things to say about this new arrangement if he got his panties in a bunch about Dylan working for Hickory Livestock—his "competition." Dylan made a note to give him a call and tell him about it before he heard it through the grapevine. And who knew, maybe if things took off, his uncle could also provide more bulls to the women's organization as well as the men's. At least until they merged into one, if that ever came about.

"When can I start?" Dylan asked.

Chapter Eight

Amarillo, TX—May

LEANN LOVED THE start of rodeo season. The potential made her giddy with excitement. The smell of freshly popped popcorn was just as much a part of her memories as the earthy smell of horse manure and saddle oil. The WPRC had selected her to bear the Texas flag during the opening ceremonies. It was an honor that she and Garth took very seriously. Her parents had given her a pair of brand-new Sierra Boots to wear, in the hopes that the company would see that she used their brand and look favorably upon her sponsorship request. They drove in from their home in Paris, Texas, with her sister Loretta to watch. She appreciated their support and was glad that they would get to see her compete. They preferred watching her barrel race over bronc riding, but they were beginning to come around to that as well.

If she hadn't been a flag bearer, however, she would've worn her old boots. These pinched in the toe, and she had a feeling she was going to have blisters on the backs of her heels by the end of the day. While she waited to ride out into the arena, LeAnn looked around at the other athletes lining up. Normally, she searched for Mick so she could avoid him. But this time, he didn't even cross her mind for more than a second. She was too focused on Dylan.

He usually didn't attend the opening ceremonies. Or if he did, she never saw him. But this time, he was a flag bearer as well. And like her, he was decked out in new duds. He was carrying the company flag for the MPRC. He winked at her when he caught her looking at him.

LeAnn flushed. Had anyone seen that?

Dylan gave her a smoky glance and a sexy smile that she felt down to her pinched toes. His knowing look and his slow, seductive appraisal of her almost made her drop the flag from her nerveless fingers. She really had to get it together if they were going to be training on a bull that weighed almost as much as her horse, if not more. It would be dangerous to let herself be distracted by a panty-melting grin and a rock-solid set of shoulders.

After the national anthem and a couple of speeches from the heads of the WPRC and the MPRC, the rodeo season was firmly underway. The men's bull-riding event was first, so LeAnn didn't have a chance to talk to Dylan and wish him luck. The rodeo was a weekend affair, so they would have plenty of time to practice tonight and tomorrow night.

As LeAnn was returning Garth to the barn because their barrel-racing event wasn't until later this afternoon, her sister Dolly came running up to her.

"Come with me and don't ask any questions."

Once Garth was secured, Dolly grabbed her upper arm and dragged her out of the barn at a fast clip, heading down toward the pens where the bulls were being kept.

"What's going on?" LeAnn said.

"I need you to be honest with me," Dolly said. "How serious are you about bull riding?"

Not this again. "Very serious. This isn't some half-assed attempt to talk me out of it, is it?"

"Just the opposite." Dolly dragged her to where the bull riders were gathered in the back of the chute.

Standing apart from them was Muriel Degas. She was a bronc rider like LeAnn, but Muriel was dressed up in leather chaps, with a bull rider chest protector and a helmet.

"What the heck is going on here?" LeAnn asked.

"The WPRC is going to announce the event in a more spectacular fashion than I had thought," Dolly said, pointing at Muriel. "She's going to compete in the men's event. There's the first women's bull rider. She's going to go last, and after she gets off the bull, that's when they're going to make the announcement."

"That's not fair," LeAnn said. "Why Muriel? Why not me?"

"Apparently, you were keeping your secret too secret. But that doesn't matter right now. What matters is you're going on after Muriel."

"I am?"

"Well," Dolly said. "I have to clear it with the MPRC and the WPRC first. While I do that, you need to grab your gear from the truck."

"I don't want to steal her thunder," LeAnn said. Sure, she was disappointed that she wouldn't be the first female bull rider in an event, but that didn't matter as long as at the end of the season she was number one.

"Don't think of it as stealing. Think of it as sharing. We can't miss the buzz this opportunity will give us," Dolly said. "Unless you're not up for this. If you're not ready, let me know now and I won't try to get you in."

Excitement jingled up and down LeAnn's spine. "Of course, I'm ready for it. You can even ask Dylan. He thinks so too."

"All right then. I'll go make the arrangements. We've got about half an hour to set this up. Go get ready and try not to let anyone see you in the gear."

After Dolly hurried away, LeAnn sprinted to the truck and grabbed her duffel bag with her protective gear and rope. She couldn't believe this was actually happening. She should really give her parents a heads-up first. Checking her phone, she didn't have much time. Calling them, she got both their voicemails. Should she break the news via text? Or should she wuss out and have Dolly tell them? When she returned to the back of the bull-riding chute where all the cowboys waited for their turn, Muriel was pretending not to hear the curious whispers from the men.

"How long have you known you were going to do this?" LeAnn asked, coming up to her.

"A couple of weeks," Muriel said. "Are you going to compete too?"

"Yes. Should be fun."

"Definitely interesting." Muriel gave the bull riders a significant glance.

LeAnn was just happy Mick wasn't standing in that crowd. "Do you know any other women who are going to compete with us?"

"Not for sure," Muriel said. "But if I had to guess, I'd say there's going to be about ten of us altogether."

That was a decent list. She had thought about half that. But ten worked for her.

"Which bull do they have you on?" LeAnn asked.

Muriel pointed to a white bull with black spots. "Pecos Bull," she said. "He's new. I don't think he's been in any event before. I might be his first rider."

"That can't be right," LeAnn said. "How will you know how he's going to react with you on his back?"

"He'll react the same as any other bull, I'd imagine." Muriel shrugged. "He's had training dummies strapped to him."

"Yeah, but they only weigh about thirty-five pounds."

"I guess we'll find out in the arena," Muriel said.

"I guess we will. Have you ever gone eight seconds before?"

"Of course, I have. The WPRC wouldn't have chosen me to be their first rider, if I hadn't," Muriel scoffed.

"Who at the WPRC chose you?" And why hadn't they approached her first?

"Shelby Miller, the CEO."

"She just called you out of the blue?"

"Yeah, pretty much.

"Well, good luck." LeAnn was going to have to sic Dolly on Shelby to see why she had called Muriel instead of her. Muriel was a decent barrel racer, but as far as LeAnn could remember, she had never placed higher than third in the bronc category.

"You too," Muriel said.

Then LeAnn saw Mick get in line to ride, and did an about-face, hurrying away before he could see her. There was no sign of Dolly anywhere, so LeAnn slipped into the stands to watch the bull riders, scanning the crowd for her parents. No luck there. She hoped that Mick got knocked on his fat head, but he scored decently. Then it was Dylan's turn.

"Kick his ass," she said under her breath.

Dylan's first bull was appropriately named Maniac, and he went out of the chute like he was possessed. Dylan was tossed back and forth, almost getting knocked off when Maniac dropped, kicked and spun. But he managed to hold firm for the full eight seconds, and jumped off the bull gracefully. The bull was still kicking up his back legs as Dylan waved to the crowd and jogged toward the exit. LeAnn ran down to meet him and got there as he was taking off his helmet.

But before LeAnn could approach him, Muriel leapt into his arms and planted a kiss on his lips.

What the...? LeAnn stopped dead in her tracks.

It didn't stop the flood of jealousy that flared through her when Dylan gently, but firmly removed Muriel's arms from around his neck and stepped back.

"Nice ride," Muriel said.

"Thanks." He squinted up at the scoreboard. He was in third, but the good news was he'd scored higher than Mick.

"Want another one?" Muriel said seductively.

"No thanks," he said, and politely stepped aside.

Muriel's gaze locked on his ass as Dylan walked away.

It was a great view, so LeAnn probably shouldn't blame her, but she did.

"He's just your trainer," LeAnn told herself, but she couldn't shake wanting to put a rock in Muriel's boot. Because she was so focused on trying to figure out why she had any right at all to these feeling, she didn't see Mick until he came up alongside of her.

Great. Just great. Just what she needed.

"Hey, Killer," Mick said, flashing her a grin that used to make her smile. Now, it just made her sick to her stomach.

"Hey, Mick," she said flatly, scanning the crowd for any signs of Dolly.

He cleared his throat. LeAnn cocked an eyebrow at him. This ought to be good.

"You're looking really hot."

"I know," she said, adjusting her tone so she sounded bored.

Mick blinked a couple times. "Don't you think that's a little conceited?"

"You just told me I looked hot."

"Y-yeah," he stuttered. "But you're supposed to thank me for the compliment."

"I agreed with you. Isn't that the same thing?"

"It sounded a little conceited."

"Conceited or confident?"

"Anyway," Mick said, appearing desperate to change the subject, "after I win this event today, why don't you and I go out for dinner?"

"So if you don't win the event, we're not going to dinner?" LeAnn said.

"No. That's not what I meant."

"That's what you said. Shouldn't you be more concerned about your second ride?" LeAnn asked.

Mick nodded. "Yeah, you're right. We'll talk after."

"We just might," LeAnn said, hoping that her score would beat his so she could cram it up his ass. But considering his bull was probably going to be a higher rank than hers, it was a long shot. Still, a girl could dream. She hoped Mick would take a hint and leave, but he lingered, like a stale fart.

"You got something to say?" she asked, seeing Dolly approach out of the corner of her eye. Mick didn't know, but it was about to get ugly if he was still around when Dolly got here. She wouldn't get violent, but she'd eviscerate him with words and film it for social media.

"I'm trying to be nice to you. We were good together. We could still be good together."

LeAnn couldn't believe she ever thought that smile he was giving her was sexy.

"You need to walk away, right now."

"Why are you being such a bitch?"

Oh no, he did not just say that.

"I'm on my period," she said flatly.

Mick jumped back as if she had shot him. "Oh God, Jesus Christ. That's awful. You don't say shit like that to a man." He backed away from her, and then hurried away.

LeAnn snort-laughed.

"What's so damn funny?" Dolly asked.

"Just dealing with an idiot."

"I've got bad news," Dolly said.

LeAnn sobered up immediately. "They don't want me to ride, do they?"

"Nope." Dolly shook her head. "They said it would take away from the announcement."

"Shit," LeAnn said. "They're wrong. They may not be able to compare Muriel's scores with the men, depending on what bull they put her on. But they could compare my score with Muriel's. It could be the start of a friendly rivalry. It would get buzz."

"It would," Dolly agreed. "But they're not on board with it. I'm sorry. Don't worry, if you're committed to being the best bull rider the WPRC, I'll put everything I've got behind making you the most popular athlete in the event."

"I know you will."

"Just not today." Dolly gave her a quick hug. "Besides, Mom and Dad are going to freak when they announce the new event."

Guilt tugged at her. "Should I tell them I'm planning on riding?"

"No," Dolly said. "They'll just rile you up and you need to concentrate on your barrel racing. But you're going to want to have the talk with them tonight. I recommend you do it before going to your training session with Dylan. That way you have a graceful way to exit the conversation if it gets heated."

"Do you think it will?" LeAnn asked.

"Yeah," Dolly said. "It was hard enough getting Mom on board for the broncs."

LeAnn remembered.

"Do you want me to tell Reba? That way we can act as a united front against Mom and Dad."

"Do you think Reba would side with us over them?"

"It doesn't have to be an us versus them, you know," Dolly said. "But yes, I know Reba will support you. She knows stuff like this is really what you want to do."

LeAnn loved her sisters and felt bad for every little annoyance that she'd let creep under her skin these past couple years.

"You could tell her. But I'll take care of Mom and Dad on my own. I do appreciate the support, though."

Dolly sagged in relief. "Good. In that case, Reba and I are going to go out to the movies tonight. Give us a call when it's safe to come home."

LeAnn chuckled.

"Good luck in the barrel-racing event."

"Don't need luck. I've got skill." LeAnn remembered Dylan had said that to her once.

Dolly rolled her eyes.

Maybe LeAnn *was* a little conceited. But she didn't need luck to score high in barrel racing. She needed luck convincing the gate man and the crew that the WPRC had authorized her to ride after Muriel. Luck and fast talking. That's how she would do it.

"I'm going to stay here and watch Dylan," LeAnn said.

"Okay, I'll see you later." Dolly was back on her phone as soon as she turned around.

LeAnn just hoped Dolly would understand. Because she was going to ride a bull tonight—regardless of what anyone said.

Chapter Nine

AFTER DYLAN'S SECOND ride, LeAnn made sure she was out there front and center. Muriel must have been busy preparing for her ride because she wasn't in sight.

"I'm going to ride after Muriel," LeAnn blurted out before he could say anything.

"What?" He froze in his tracks, and stared at her in horror.

"Oh," LeAnn said. *He must not have known about Muriel.* "Muriel Degas is going to be the last bull rider today. That's how the WPRC is going to announce the new event."

"Yeah," Dylan said. "I heard about that last night, but I didn't think you were going to ride as well."

Wait, what? Distracted, LeAnn had to replay his words in her head. "You knew Muriel was going ride today? Why didn't you tell me?" LeAnn wasn't sure if she was hurt or pissed.

"I didn't want you to worry about it."

"You don't get to make that call," she said, identifying the emotion she was feeling as betrayal.

"I chose not to tell you so you would find out about it like everyone else and be surprised."

"I was surprised all right. Surprised they picked your girlfriend instead of me." Shit. She hadn't meant to say that.

Dylan made a face. "She's not my girlfriend."

"She looked awfully friendly with you."

Sighing, Dylan unhooked his chest protection. "We have a history."

"Ancient history?" LeAnn asked.

"It's in the past. And I'm not planning on letting history repeat itself. Why? Are you interested in a little history lesson?" Dylan stepped in closer to her and LeAnn forgot how to breathe.

Damn, she wanted to kiss him.

Focus.

"My ride. It's all last-minute," LeAnn said nervously, her hands shaking. She hated lying like this, but this was her shot and she had to take it. "Because it's all still so secretive, I need your help getting me a bull."

"I didn't think that was going to start up so soon," Dylan said. "A little warning would have been nice."

LeAnn wasn't sure what he was talking about, but she nodded. "Sorry."

"I don't like putting you in the arena before we could train more," he said, his face grim. "Are you sure you need to do this?"

Was she? She swallowed hard. "It's not the first time I've been on a bull. Trent Campbell trained me, remember?"

"This isn't what we decided last night, though," he said. "I haven't had time to vet any of these bulls."

"Vet?"

"Not like Reba. I mean I haven't had time to look them over. We were going to take it slow."

"That was before I knew they had slated Muriel for this exhibition ride," LeAnn said.

"True. They did mention you had been considered." He rubbed his jaw. "I don't like it, though."

His words threw her again. "Who mentioned me? Shelby Miller?"

"No, I was with the Jackson Blevins, the CEO of the MPRC last night."

All the alphabet soup of letters was making her head spin. "He wanted me to ride?" LeAnn perked up at the thought.

"Yeah, so I suppose he talked to Shelby about it."

"What were you doing talking with the head honcho about me last night?" she asked.

"We were talking about bulls and your name came up. Hickory Livestock offered me a job selecting which of their bulls to send to the WPRC this season."

That was perfect. "Can you find me a bull to ride?"

"Yeah." Dylan nodded. "Mr. Hickory has some here. I haven't had much time to look at them yet, but we'll find you a good one."

"That's good," she said, wringing her hands. Looking around, she hoped that she'd be able to get away with this. She didn't want to be left out when the announcement was made. She wanted to be part of history, and this was her shot at it.

Dylan went up to one of the cowboys and said, "I need

another bull like the one they gave Muriel ready to go in the chute right after her ride."

The cowboy looked up with interest. "Oh really? Why?"

LeAnn gave him a big smile. "Because I'll be riding after Muriel."

The cowboy squinted at Dylan. "Are you sure about this?"

"Not my call. This is coming from the higher-ups."

A flash of guilt nearly had LeAnn changing her mind. She didn't want to get anyone in trouble. Not Dolly, not this cowboy, and certainly not Dylan. "I'll take full responsibility." And she would too. She'd come clean and tell anyone who wanted to reprimand them that she had bamboozled them.

The cowboy still didn't look convinced, but LeAnn was desperate. She had come too far to let this slip through her fingers now. "While the crowd is still reacting to Muriel being the first woman bull rider in this rodeo series—" that had been harder to get out than LeAnn would have thought "—they want to give her someone to be compared to. And that's me."

"Are you sure?" the cowboy said. "Muriel doesn't have any other events today. And I know that you're barrel racing later."

Oh yeah, she had briefly forgotten about that. "I'm sure," LeAnn said, even though she wasn't. *Great.* Now, she was second-guessing herself about what she had just set in motion.

You know who does shit like this? Who lies to get his own

way? Who uses people? That voice in her head asked viciously. LeAnn heard Mick's laugh, like a demented hyena.

"I can't do this," she whispered.

But no one heard her. And she didn't have the courage to say it again. This was how things got done in the rodeo. Nice girls finished last. Merry Grayson taught her that. You had to stand out if you wanted the big sponsors. And nobody stood out by meekly following the rules. If you wanted to succeed in a man's world, you had to be ruthless. LeAnn rubbed her stomach, which churned with acid. The end justified the means, didn't it?

"Okay," the cowboy said. "Do you have a preference?" He directed the question to Dylan.

"Which one is Muriel riding?"

"She's riding Pecos Bull. He's got potential. In a few years, you might be facing him down."

"Is he your best bull?" LeAnn asked.

"In his category."

LeAnn wasn't familiar with the categories. She'd research that later. "Who's the second best?"

"That would be Whiplash."

"I'll take him," LeAnn said.

"There's probably a reason why his name is Whiplash," Dylan said.

"Yeah," LeAnn said snarkily. "Usually, they don't name bulls Fluffy Bunny Kitten Pants."

"She's got a point," the cowboy said. "However, can you imagine how much of a bitch it would be to lose to a bull named Fluffy Bunny Kitten Pants?"

"What's the bull's track record?" Dylan asked.

"Same as Pecos Bull. This is his first event with a rider on his back."

Dylan didn't look convinced. LeAnn couldn't blame him. He was probably thinking the same thing that she'd said to Muriel about Pecos Bull. You never knew what a first-time bull would do. But that was also the challenge, the fun of it.

"Oh what a coincidence, this is my first event too," LeAnn said. "He's perfect."

While they got Whiplash together, LeAnn headed over to the announcer's table. She needed to talk to someone who would understand how important this was to her. LeAnn waited for a break and caught Merry Grayson's eye. Waving her over, LeAnn looked around to make sure no one was watching them.

"Hey, Killer, what's up?" Merry said, opening a can of soda and taking a long drink. "I wish this was beer. But the WPRC and the MPRC kinda frown on drinking while on duty."

LeAnn smiled at Merry's obvious annoyance. "That's poor working conditions right there."

"What can I do for you? I hate to rush you, but I only have a few moments."

Taking a shaky breath, LeAnn said, "I'm assuming you heard about Muriel Degas."

"Yeah, ain't that a kick in the ass? We just got handed a new sheet with all of her stats on it so we can talk her up."

LeAnn bit her lip, wondering if she should take the chance and tell Merry what she was planning to do.

"Do you have something to say, LeAnn?" Merry asked

with a grin.

"I'm riding after Muriel on a bull named Whiplash."

"I haven't gotten a stat sheet on you." She leaned against the post and crossed her arms.

"Well, that's probably because no one knows about it but me and a few others in the bull pen."

"Good for you," Merry said.

LeAnn blinked. "You mean it?"

"Shit yeah. Why the hell not?"

"I'm worried that someone might get in trouble," she said. "I'm almost ready to call this whole thing off, but I want it so much I can taste it."

"Then go for it. Trust me. No one is going to get in trouble. You should see some of the pranks these guys pull on each other. As long as the crowd is entertained and no one gets hurt, the MPRC won't care."

"What about the WPRC?"

"With the shit they've pulled in the past, they won't even blink at this. Can you go eight seconds?"

"Definitely."

"Then go for it. I'll make sure the crowd knows you're a pro."

"Thanks, Merry," LeAnn said, clutching her arm. "I was hoping you'd say that."

"You owe me a beer."

"Deal."

"Good luck."

"Thanks." LeAnn felt a lot better about this.

MOST OF THE bull riders had moved on after their final scores, especially if they were not in the top three. The last male rider got tossed off without staying on the full eight seconds. As the staff cleared the arena to set up for Muriel, Merry and the other announcers kept the crowd interested.

"We have a special ride right now that wasn't on your schedule. I'd like to take the time to introduce you to a new cowboy or should I say, cow*girl*," one of the male announcers said.

LeAnn rolled her eyes.

"Cowgirl? How about athlete?" Merry said.

It was nice to know she hadn't lost her snarky attitude. Merry launched into Muriel's record for bronc riding and her history with the WPRC.

"Yeah, but bull riding is a men's sport," the male announcer said.

"Well, let's just see about that," Merry retorted. "Y'all said that about bronc riding, but if my memory serves me, Rod, I smoked your scores when we were on the same horse."

The crowd responded with jeers, hoots and laughs. A part of LeAnn wished that she was in the audience right now, watching Muriel ride the bull. But there would be someone filming it and she could review it on YouTube later. Right now, she had to get herself settled on her own bull.

"You got this," Dylan said, giving her a quick hug.

She nodded, wishing she could cling to him a little bit longer, but she didn't have a lot of time. He felt good and solid and, for a moment, she almost changed her mind. But then she forced herself to step away from Dylan and check the straps on her helmet and chest protector.

This was her destiny. This was her show now. She could do this.

LeAnn watched as they walked Whiplash into the chute. When he was settled, she held on to each side of the chute and slowly lowered herself onto his back, taking care not to touch him with her spurs. Sliding the flank strap down and around him, LeAnn was surprised that her hands were shaking. She was struck with a case of nerves that didn't make any damned sense to her. She hadn't felt this way when she rode a bronc for the first time in front of a rodeo crowd. She didn't even freak out when she rode a bull for the first time. So why was she having second thoughts now?

"Any last-minute advice?" she asked Dylan.

"Lose your feet, lose your seat," he said, invoking the bull rider's mantra.

She tightened her thighs around the bull. LeAnn gripped the rope, and a quiver of something that felt like fear went through her stomach. He was bigger than the bulls she was used to.

She registered the crowd's approval at Muriel's ride. They liked her.

"Knock 'em dead, Killer," the cowboy who had brought in Whiplash said.

"Killer?" She heard Mick's voice. "What the hell is she doing on that bull? Get her down from there."

Why the hell did he think he had a say in anything she did? LeAnn wondered.

"I'll handle him," Dylan said grimly and hopped down from the chute to confront Mick.

"Now, folks, it looks like we're not done with surprises today," Merry said, with admiration in her voice.

LeAnn grinned.

"We've got a second female rider in the chute, which is not only a surprise for you but also for everyone else. This rider heard that Muriel was competing today and decided to throw her hat in the ring as well."

She groaned. *Thanks a lot, Merry.*

"Don't let anyone tell you that a woman can't ride a bull. If you liked Muriel, you're going to love to see what this rider can do. And you're not going to believe who it is. Or maybe you would. Ladies and gentlemen, LeAnn 'Killer' Keller."

Then there was no more time for fear, for thinking about Mick, Dylan, Muriel or anything else in her head. She nodded to the gate man, and off they went.

Oh shit!

LeAnn knew she only had to stay on for eight seconds. Eight seconds in the real world was nothing. It was a few heartbeats. It was a blink. Hell, it took longer than that to pour a cup of coffee. Right now, though, eight seconds seemed like forever. Whiplash made Apis look like Garth. This bull was pissed. All she could think of was that she couldn't wreck on her first ride. Maybe she should have waited for the actual event. Maybe she should have waited for a seasoned bull. Or one that was smaller.

Whiplash's hooves barely touched the ground. He jumped. He twisted. He bucked. He did everything possible to throw her off. LeAnn's wrist hurt from gripping the rope so tight. Her other arm that was wildly trying to help her stay balanced felt like it was dislocated. She couldn't touch the bull with it. She'd lose all her points.

Her thighs screamed at her as she fought hard to stay on. Her backbone ached as it slammed down on the bull not once, but twice. She could not stay on for a moment longer. She didn't know if it had been eight seconds, six seconds, or just one long second. She hadn't heard the buzzer over the roar of the crowd and the roaring in her own head. Then she was airborne.

At times like this, LeAnn wished she was a cat because she knew she wasn't going to land on her feet. It always happened in slow motion, and she heard Trent's voice tell her how to fall. Tucking her shoulders, she rolled as she hit the ground. Somehow, she used the momentum to get back up on her feet and threw her hands up in the air in victory. LeAnn knew she would feel the pain later. But right now, all that mattered was that she had done it.

Or had she?

Dylan was there helping her out of the arena. The bull-fighters had done their job and had kept Whiplash far away from her.

"You lied to me," Dylan said, his face tight with fury.

She had to take a step back from the emotions rolling off him. "I'm sorry," LeAnn said.

"Are you all right?" Dylan growled.

"Yeah, just a little shaky," she said, feeling guilty as hell.

"You scared the hell out of me." He yanked her into his arms.

She sagged into him, clutching him hard. "I'm okay."

"You could have been killed."

"That's a little dramatic," she said, lifting her head up to look at him, but his eyes were far away. "I'm okay."

Dylan snapped back from wherever he had gone. "I know. I know." He gave a shaky sigh. "I've got to get better at this."

"Did I do it?" she asked, feeling like she was out of her body looking down.

"You didn't make the full eight," Dylan said.

Disappointment stabbed her deep in the heart. Shit. She had wanted to come out with authority. "It would have gone over better if I had."

"You had one hell of a ride, but that bull was too much for you."

Stung, she glared up at him. But she didn't see any condescension or criticism in his eyes. It was what it was. Okay, maybe Whiplash had been too much bull for her.

"Did Muriel stay on?"

"Yes."

Shit again.

LeAnn deflated. It didn't matter that Muriel probably had the easier bull, not at the moment anyway. "I wanted to beat Mick's time," she said softly.

"That was what this was about?" Dylan asked, his jaw dropping.

"Part of it," she said. "Part of it was my own ego."

"Don't beat yourself up. We all do stupid shit now and then."

"So you're not mad at me?" she asked hopefully.

"No. I'm still very pissed at you and we're going to talk about it later, once I can speak without shouting at you."

"Oh," she said in a small voice.

Dylan guided her back to the barn and helped her get out of her gear. "How's that shoulder? You landed hard on it."

"The adrenaline is still running," LeAnn said. "But I'm going to feel it later."

"Better get ahead of it," Dylan said, handing her two ibuprofen and a bottle of water. "It wasn't a bad ride. You handled whatever Whiplash threw at you well. There are a few things we can work on, but I think you can give Muriel and anyone else who decides to join you in this a run for their money."

"How did you do?" LeAnn asked.

"Third place."

"You'll get 'em next time," she said, linking her fingers through his.

He stared down at them, but didn't say anything.

"I wish I could've stayed on the full eight seconds," she said, liking the warmth and comfort she got simply by holding his hand. She could use another hug, but she didn't want to push her luck. He had a right to be pissed at her.

"A lot of cowboys don't go the eight seconds. A lot of cowboys wouldn't have been able to stay on that bull. There's no shame in that. Maybe you'll get another chance to ride Whiplash—once I'm done evaluating him."

Dylan always knew what to say to make her feel better.

Her sisters stormed into the barn.

"Are you all right?" Reba said, taking her by the arms and turning her around.

"Just dizzy from you spinning me like that. Knock it off. I'm fine."

"I told you they said no," Dolly said between her teeth.

"I gave Muriel plenty of time. The impact was still there, and the crowd was on board. I just gave them a little extra."

"And you," Dolly said, whirling on Dylan. "You're supposed to be her trainer. You're supposed to keep her safe."

"She's safe," Dylan said. "I will admit, it was too much bull for her at this point, but your sister handled it fine."

She hated that Dylan felt the need to stick up for her. "Don't blame Dylan. This was all my idea. I hoodwinked him and everybody else."

Reba spoke over her. "Fine? You weren't sitting next to our parents when she came out of that chute."

LeAnn winced.

"I don't have a lot of experience dealing with parents at rodeo events, but I expect it was a bit of a shock to them."

Dolly gave a little laugh that didn't have a trace of humor in it. "That's putting it gently, yes."

"I'd better go talk to them," LeAnn said.

"Not here. Not now," Dolly said. "You're coming with me. We have a PR storm going on right now. You caught the WPRC with their pants down. You're going to have to make it right." Dolly grabbed her by the arm and tugged her along. Reba gave Dylan one final glare before following them.

Chapter Ten

DYLAN WENT STRAIGHT back to his hotel room after the rodeo. He was glad he'd splurged on it but was even happier he had won his bulldogging event so he wouldn't have to feel guilty about forking over the money. After taking a long, hot shower, he should have felt better. While he was clean, he was also still torqued at LeAnn. She'd reminded him of Johnny Montana today. Full of piss and vinegar and to hell with the rules.

It had killed Johnny. He wasn't going to let it kill LeAnn as well. But he wasn't sure how he was going to stop it. Dylan felt like he was on a runaway train and couldn't find the brakes. That damned bull had been too much for her. If she had given him time, he could have picked one that was more suited to her skill level. As much as LeAnn thought she was an expert rider, she didn't have the experience that Muriel had.

Muriel had told him that she had been riding bulls even before she was riding broncs. She had even competed down in Mexico, which impressed the hell out of him because the bulls down there tended to be a lot meaner and harder to ride. Still, he had to face the fact that he had a bit of a bias toward LeAnn. He didn't care if Mick, Muriel, or hell, even himself wrecked on a bull and took a bump that left bruises. It bothered him that LeAnn might have gotten hurt. It was stupid, overprotective, and everything that he shouldn't feel. But it was still there, along with the memories of Johnny Montana's last ride.

Dylan thought about hitting the gym to get rid of some of the anxiety, but his knees and his back ached too much. He wanted to soak in the hot tub, but he didn't want to be alone and he didn't want any company that wasn't LeAnn. So he was fucked. He flopped down on the bed instead.

What a shitshow today had been.

At least Jackson Blevins had thought LeAnn's stunt was hysterical, but he'd admonished Dylan to give him a heads-up next time. Well, there had better fucking not be a next time. But rather than tell Jackson that LeAnn had broadsided him too, he went along with it.

Stretching out, Dylan closed his eyes and tried to rest. But the events of the day kept him from finding peace. There was that thing with LeAnn, sure. And Lola wasn't performing at her prime either. But it was the other animals that he saw that gnawed on his insides. There were horses in worse shape than Lola giving it their all out there. If he could just get his horse rescue ranch project up and running, Dylan could offer the owners a choice to give their animals a little peace in their retirement.

He rubbed his knees. It was getting close to his retirement too. His back and knees ached more than they used to.

When his phone rang and he saw it was his uncle, he almost didn't answer it. But then he remembered that he'd never gotten around to telling him about his new job with Hickory Livestock. Uncle Lou should hear it from him.

"Yeah," he said.

"Saw you on the TV today," Lou said. "You were stinking up the joint."

"Yeah, thanks for noticing." Dylan put his arm over his eyes.

"Do you know the two cuties on the bulls?"

"Yeah, both of them. As a matter of fact, they were on Hickory Livestock's bulls and I got a job with Hickory to choose which bulls are going to the WPRC."

"You're going to recommend mine, right?"

Dylan snorted. He knew that was coming. "Since Hickory Livestock is paying my salary, I'm pretty sure they want me to funnel their bulls to the women's league. But don't worry," he said before his uncle could protest, "I know that Jackson Blevins is very happy with the quality of bulls you're providing for the men. Who knows, you may be able to branch out to the women's league sooner rather than later."

"Just keep me in mind."

"I will," Dylan said. "How's Paint?" Paint was his uncle's workhorse, who had seen better days.

"Gone."

Dylan's hands clenched into fists. Paint hadn't deserved to go to the slaughterhouse, but that's where Lou had been planning on sending him once his working days were over.

If only he had his rescue set up.

"I wish you would have waited," Dylan said, trying not to shout.

"For what?"

"I've got applications for a bank loan pending and there is a farm coming up on auction that might work out for the rescue ranch I have in mind."

Lou scoffed. "You're not going to be up and running this year, even if you do get the loan and the ranch."

"You still could have waited."

"I'm not running a charity. That's your dream. You might want to run the idea by your father, you know. He's part of that *Shark Tank* wannabe organization that's looking to invest in new ideas."

"No thanks," Dylan said. "My father has made it very clear that he thinks I ruined my life by going into rodeo. I don't need him to shit all over this idea as well."

"That's just because he's worried about you," Lou said. "You're the only kid he's got left."

"He's got a funny way of showing it," Dylan said. This wasn't a new argument. His uncle was always trying to find excuses for the way Dylan's parents had foisted him off on them.

"You should call them anyway. They were asking about you the other day."

"The phone works both ways," Dylan said.

"Stubborn. Anyway, the reason why I called is I need to make sure you're going to work on the ranch during the off-season. I'm buying a few hundred more bulls and I need the extra help."

If Dylan's loan came through, he'd be too busy to help his uncle. But a pang of guilt kept him from refusing. He'd make it work. "Yeah, sure. You can count on me."

"I'd better," Lou said gruffly.

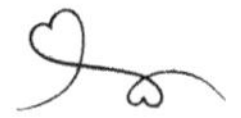

LEANN DIDN'T GET a chance to talk to her parents until after the rodeo. She had what she was going to say to them all planned out. In fact, she had been practicing the speech in her head ever since she'd decided to do this. She knew what her parents would say and she had a response to counter every argument they raised. Mostly it would be the same conversation they had when she'd told them she wanted to ride broncs, only with a little bit more emphasis on the danger.

But she'd been absolutely blown away when she walked into the Winnebago and saw her parents staring into their beers, looking haggard and ten years older.

"I'm sorry if I worried you," LeAnn said, hesitantly.

Her mother whirled on her, angrier than LeAnn had ever seen her. Tears shimmered in her eyes. Her mouth was compressed in a tight line and her hands shook. "Worried? You scared us to death."

"I've been practicing and training. I wouldn't have gotten on that bull unless I knew how to ride." She sighed, realizing they wouldn't care. "I know you don't agree with my choice to ride bulls, but it's just like my choice to ride the broncs. I know what I'm doing and I'm good at it. I like it. And this is an opportunity to advance my career."

"You don't have a career," her mother said. "You can play around in the rodeo for another few years and then get a real job like I did. Like your sisters did."

"Mom, this is my real job."

"Is that right? This not a career. You have a shelf life. How many fifty-year-old rodeo stars do you know?"

"There's not a lot," LeAnn said, trying her hardest not to act defensive.

"You can't ride bulls for the rest of your life."

"No, but I can ride bulls now, save the money I'm making, maybe invest it."

"Invest in what?" her father said, speaking for the first time. He sounded weary and tired, and she hated hearing the defeat in his voice.

"I don't know. I haven't thought that far ahead."

"And that's the problem," he said. "You don't think things through. You're too young to make any type of life decisions."

"I have time."

"Not if you keep doing dangerous things like this," her father said.

"It's not worth risking your life," her mother said.

"I'm good at what I do. My life wasn't at risk."

"You couldn't stay on the bull for eight seconds," her father said. "You're not that good. And you can't tell me that riding that bull didn't screw up your performance in barrel racing afterwards. You barely placed."

LeAnn sucked in a breath. She had come in fourth when she should have won the event. "I am sorry you feel that way," she said. "And I'm so sorry that I hurt you both. I was wrong. This is a hard lesson that I'm learning right now. But I understand and respect your decision and I want to thank you for all the support you have given me over the years. I wouldn't be here right now without you."

"This would've been so much easier if you stayed in the beauty pageants," her mother said tearfully.

"Easy isn't really my strong point," LeAnn said.

Her father snorted.

"Boy oh boy, did you fuck up," her oldest sister Loretta said, when LeAnn walked out of the Winnebago to get some air. She, Reba and Dolly had started a fire in the fire pit and were sitting around it. They were close enough to have heard her parents lay into her.

"Tell me something I don't know," LeAnn said, getting up to give her oldest sister a big hug. And if she held on too long and too tight, Loretta didn't mention it.

"They'll get over it," Loretta said, hugging her back. "I have to thank you, though, for taking my place as family pariah. I thought because I was divorced and homeless, I was going to have to wear that mantle for a couple more years."

Loretta sometimes acted like a second mother, but it was times like this, when she acted like a co-conspirator, that made LeAnn appreciate her all the more.

"Always glad to help out," LeAnn said.

"Tell me all about the bull riding. Was it worth it?"

"It wasn't worth causing Mom and Dad this much pain. But I love bull riding. I want to win this. And I'm going to have the time of my life doing it."

"You don't have to look so miserable about it," Loretta said.

"At least the WPRC wasn't too pissed by your little stunt," Dolly said. "They came around when they saw that they were trending on Twitter and going viral on TikTok."

"You could have told me what was going on," Reba grumbled. "Both of you."

"I'm sorry," LeAnn said. She wanted a good cry, but she supposed that could wait until her parents had left and she had the Winnebago to herself for a while. There was one more person, though, that she needed to apologize to. She wouldn't even blame him if he didn't answer when she texted.

You around?

Even though she didn't deserve it, he replied right away.

Yup.

Can I call?

Sure.

"I've got to make a phone call. Don't leave until I get back," LeAnn said to Loretta.

"No promises." Loretta craned her neck. "They want to get on the road sooner rather than later."

"I'll stall them," Reba said. "Make your phone call quick and then say your goodbyes."

"Thanks." LeAnn walked away from the RV, appreciating the cool night breeze. "Hey," she said when Dylan picked up. "I'm just checking in. Did you get in trouble?"

"There were words exchanged," Dylan said. "But we all came to an understanding."

"What was the understanding?"

"That women are crazy. You in particular."

Ouch. Yet she deserved that, so she would take the lumps. "Can I see you tonight?"

There was a long pause and she thought he'd tell her to

go pound sand, but then he said, "I'm staying at the Holiday Inn on Main Street. Room 402."

"I'll be there in about an hour," she said, and then because she couldn't think of anything she wanted to say over the phone, she hung up.

Saying goodbye to her parents was a frosty and uncomfortable affair. They flinched away from her offered hugs and got into the car without looking back at her.

"They'll come around," Loretta said, giving her an extra-long hug to make up for it.

"Yeah," LeAnn sniffled.

But the dust hadn't settled on their car leaving the parking lot, when LeAnn headed for the truck. "I'm going out. Don't wait up."

"Don't drink tonight," Reba said.

"I won't." LeAnn had other things in mind for tonight. Nerves made her jittery as she drove into town and walked into the Holiday Inn. She wanted to make things right with Dylan, but that wasn't the only reason she was here. LeAnn wanted him to hold her and tell her they were okay. And she wanted to kiss him again. She only hoped he didn't toss her out on her butt for lying to him today.

Dylan answered the door before she could knock. He was shirtless and his hair was sticking up, as if he had been running his hands through it.

"I wasn't sure if you were going to come."

"I wanted to face the music in person," she said, pushing by him. LeAnn resisted the urge to touch the muscles on his chest and abdomen.

"I'm still pissed," he said, closing the door.

"You have a right to be," she said. Now that she was here, alone with him, she was no longer nervous. "I'm sorry. Is there anything, any way, I could make it up to you?" For a moment, she was horrified that he would take that as a come-on, but she should have known better. He wasn't Mick.

His hard-ass stare softened and he rubbed the back of his neck wearily. "Yeah, just don't lie to me again. And as your coach, I want you to listen to me when I tell you how to become a better bull rider."

"I will," she promised.

"That means you ride the bulls I tell you to. And if I want you working on other things, you don't give me a hard time."

"I can do that," LeAnn said, relieved that he hadn't suffered for her poor decision.

She felt weepy because his reaction was so different from what she had received from her parents. She would rather chew glass, though, than let Dylan know that she was seconds away from bawling her eyes out.

"All right then. In that case, I want you to meet me at the body shop on Eighth Avenue at six in the morning tomorrow."

"Six a.m.?" LeAnn cried out, almost forgetting that she wasn't going to argue with him anymore.

"Are we going to have a problem?" he asked mildly.

"No." She'd be there.

"Don't worry, I'll go easy on you. I know you're still sore from today."

Truth was with so much else going on, she hadn't had

time to think about her aches and pains.

"Call me when you're ready, and I'll pick you up. We can have breakfast before the gym if you need to fuel up."

"You're the boss," she said.

"I could get used to hearing that."

LeAnn didn't want to go back to the Winnebago. She didn't want to leave him. Placing her hand on his shoulder, she lightly stroked up and down his arm. Her fingers tingled at the contact.

"What are you playing at?" he asked, his voice husky.

She was lost in his eyes, could spend the night just standing here. "I want you," she whispered and pressed her lips against his.

Dylan hauled her against him, kissing her roughly. She felt his anger in the way he held her, but instead of being afraid, her body thrilled to his touch. It felt wonderful to hang on to him while he ravaged her mouth. Pressing against him, LeAnn ran her hands up and down his back.

It didn't matter that he was probably still pissed at her and that she shouldn't get involved with a rodeo cowboy while she was trying to win an important event. But all that she wanted was right here and she couldn't walk out the door without experiencing the heady passion that she had almost convinced herself she had imagined. With each pass of his tongue over hers, with his hands roving all over hers, LeAnn's expectations built until she was trembling.

Her fingers dropped to the waistband of his pants.

"Sweetheart," he said raggedly, dragging his mouth from hers.

Feeling daring, she kissed down his chest, pausing to

flick her tongue over his nipples.

He groaned and tangled his fingers in her hair. Frenzied now, she kissed down the hard planes of his abdomen until she knelt before him. Slipping his cock out of his pants, she gripped him.

"You don't have to do this," Dylan said, shivering as she darted her tongue over the tip.

"I want to," she whispered and then took him in her mouth.

Pulling him deep in her throat, she slowly moved back until he almost slipped out. She sucked him long and slow until he held her head against him and rocked his hips, thrusting into her mouth. LeAnn felt powerful and desired as he took what he wanted from her. She had never been so turned on and when he came, she was close to following.

"Come here, beautiful," Dylan said, undressing her with reverence.

Shivering under his intense scrutiny, LeAnn moaned when he brushed his fingers over her nipples.

"I love how pink they are," he said, dipping his head down to taste them.

Crying out, LeAnn clung to his shoulders while he sucked on each tip and swirled his tongue down her chest to her belly.

"My turn," he said, picking her up and carrying her to the bed.

Spreading her legs, he tasted her.

"Dylan," she cried out, feeling her thighs quiver at the brush of the stubble on his cheeks.

"I'm going to take my time with you," he said, then

buried his face between her legs.

LeAnn squirmed and moaned. She choked on his name as he stroked his tongue over her clit. The room was spinning. Her entire body was throbbing. And she needed more. But he was relentless in licking her until the quaking turned into a crescendo and she moaned loud and long.

She was dimly aware that Dylan was putting on a condom.

"You're everything I've been dreaming about," he said in her ear before flipping her over on her stomach.

Moving up on her hands and knees, LeAnn groaned in satisfaction when he slid inside her from behind. When he rocked into her, she looked at him over her shoulder. "Same," she panted. "Same."

"You feel amazing," he grunted, pounding into her at a hard pace.

"Yes," she crooned, loving the way he moved inside her.

The slap of their bodies was as loud as their mutual breathing.

"Please," she said, moving back to meet him stroke for stroke. She had missed this. She had missed him. She couldn't believe she had stayed away from him, from this, for so long. She had so many regrets. She regretted never coming back for a second night. She regretted lying to him today.

But this. She could never regret being here with him like this.

"Come for me, baby," he said, his voice strained.

She knew he was flying as high as she was. "Come with

me," LeAnn begged.

He gave a soft laugh. "Always."

Her entire body clenched as the orgasm crashed over her and took him with her.

Dylan held her as their heartbeats slowed back to normal. He kissed her shoulder and then rolled away to dispose of the condom. She felt boneless and when he came back to bed, she was powerless to do anything but let him tuck her in next to him.

They kissed slowly this time, enjoying each other. LeAnn caressed his back, indulgently. Their legs intertwined, and their bodies fit together perfectly.

I want this for always, she thought. Not just for tonight. But she refused to dwell on it. She had made the decision to come here, to be with him. There were no strings attached to their lovemaking.

Eventually, the heat built between them again. His hands massaged her breasts, and her legs opened for him. After putting on another condom, Dylan slipped inside her again. This time, they stared into each other's eyes as he rocked them both to a slow and languorous orgasm.

Afterwards, she clung to him, desperate to keep the feeling of bliss from fading away. She dozed a bit, content to be wrapped in his arms. But she woke up, tense and afraid. Had she spent the night?

When she bolted upright, she saw that the clock read midnight.

"Stay," Dylan murmured, running a hand down her back.

"I wish I could." She turned back and kissed him. So

many wishes. But before he could convince her to stay with his talented hands and tongue, she pulled away and got dressed. "It'll be worse if I'm not there when my sisters get up. I don't want to worry them."

"I understand," he said. "Do you want me to drive you home?"

"I think I've shocked my family enough for one day." She paused in the doorway. "Thank you for forgiving me." Her voice wobbled and she hated that. Everything was hitting her all at once. She had slept with Dylan again. Did that make this a two-night stand?

"Drive safe, Killer."

"I will," LeAnn said.

"Text me when you get home."

She nodded, shivering from the sudden cold she felt. She wished she could spend the night cuddled up to him. But they didn't have that type of relationship, did they? Maybe they could.

"See you tomorrow," she said.

Chapter Eleven

DYLAN WAS MAKING LeAnn sweat and groan, only this time, they were spending a few hours in the gym. As a bit of payback for her lying to him about having permission to ride the bull, he let her stew for a few days, only allowing her on mechanical bulls and working on her core in the gym.

The WPRC needed a few more weeks to get the infrastructure settled in, so the events at Fort Worth and San Antonio wouldn't count toward rankings. But it would give the crowd a hint of things to come.

Fort Worth was going to be their dress rehearsal for the big time, so to speak, and LeAnn would be riding one of the ten bulls he had picked out from Mr. Hickory's stock. The bulls needed the practice as much as the riders did.

While she was working on her upper body strength training, Dylan got a phone call that he had been waiting on.

"I've got to take this," he said. "Keep doing the rotation. I'll be right back."

"I'm going to hold you to that," LeAnn said, blowing out a controlled breath as she pushed up on the weights. "You promised to do the elliptical with me."

"Looking forward to it," he said, answering his phone. "Yeah, this is Dylan."

"Mr. Porter, this is Sarah from Lone Star Loans. I'm afraid I don't have good news for you."

Crap.

"You didn't get the loan financed for the full amount?" he asked, hoping for the best.

"I'm sorry. Your application has been declined."

"Can you try another bank?" He kicked the wall lightly with the toe of his boot.

"We tried several. They all turned us down."

"Did they give a reason why?"

"You're still too new at your job. While it was positive to see that there will be a steady paycheck, the banks need their clients to have a more stable employment history."

"I've been paying my own bills since I was sixteen," Dylan said. Barely. But he didn't have any credit card debt. That should have counted for something.

"I know it's frustrating," she said. "But I think if you try again next year, you'll have more success."

"Yeah, thanks." He hung up. Lola didn't have another year in her. It might be time to bite the bullet. Before he could change his mind, he scrolled through to find his father's number and hit the call button.

Dylan wasn't surprised when it went to voicemail. He didn't leave a message. He thought about calling his mother, but she didn't have any financial authority. And he wasn't sure what to say to her anyway. The last time he spoke with either of them had been at Christmas. They were heading out for a party and hadn't wanted to talk for very long. Maybe it was a good thing his father hadn't answered the phone just now. Dylan didn't want to be that son who only called when he was obligated to or when he needed money. He thought about calling his uncle and asking for help, but money had always been tight for them.

"What's the matter?" LeAnn asked when he came back. She was wiping down the machine she had been on.

"Nothing," he said. "I'm going to hit the heavy bag while you finish up your circuit."

Pretending he didn't see her frown of concern, he rummaged through his bag for his boxing gloves. The first couple of punches got out some of the frustration, but then the guilt and shame hit him, and he started to sweat it out in earnest.

He didn't get the loan.

Punch.

He was going to lose out on the farm he wanted to buy at auction.

Punch.

He was closing in on thirty and his bull-riding days were numbered.

Punch.

He had no savings.

Punch.

If he had stayed on his uncle's farm, he'd be a foreman right now and making decent money.

Punch.

His horse was suffering.

Punch.

He had nothing to offer a woman like LeAnn.

Punch.

He took a breather, hands on his hips while he paced around the area. LeAnn was working on her reps and concentrating on them, so he was able to watch her without making her self-conscious. Shit, another thing in his life he couldn't have. Dylan shook his head, trying to clear it, and went back to the bag.

What was it about her that had him thinking he could be less of a disappointment in a relationship? How about everything? She was smart, pretty, and a hell of an athlete. It was easy to admire her courage, not so easy watching her determination to ride a bull and risk getting hurt.

"Did it insult your mama?" LeAnn said, when he stopped to catch his breath.

"Huh?"

"You were going at it so hard, I figured it had said something out of line."

Wiping the sweat off his forehead with a towel, he said, "Just had some bad news, that's all."

"Anything I can do to help?" she asked, concern etched on her lovely face.

"Nothing I can't handle."

"That's not what I asked."

He smiled at her. "No, but thank you."

"Why don't we go grab some lunch and talk about it?" LeAnn asked.

"Are you trying to get out of cardio?"

"You seem like you're too tuckered out to hit the elliptical."

Dylan wasn't buying her innocent look. "I'll tell you

what. The last one that gets to the three mile marker buys lunch," he said, jumping onto the machine.

"That's not fair," she cried, clambering up on the machine next to him. "You've got longer legs."

"Then you better move faster," he said, starting the machine.

"Cheater," she said, but stepped up her game.

SINCE LEANN WON by the skin of her teeth, she decided not to brag about it. But she did make him take her out for ribs and a baked potato the size of a small boulder.

"Tomorrow, we're on the bulls, right?" she asked Dylan after they'd placed their order.

"Yup."

"I'm excited to see the other women compete. There's eight of us." LeAnn wanted to see if she was better than Muriel. Fort Worth would be the first time all of them were in the arena at the same time. She hoped she did well.

"When should we start heading over to Fort Worth?" LeAnn asked. She was hoping to travel at the same time as he did so they could be on the road together and it wouldn't seem so isolated.

"I've got a few things to take care of here tomorrow. But you need to be there by Thursday."

"I can stay and wait for you. What do you have to do? I can help," she said.

"I'm working with Hickory Livestock to see which bulls are going to San Antonio the week after next."

"What about the ones for Fort Worth?"

"They're already en route."

"Do you mind if I tag along tomorrow?" she asked.

"I don't mind, but wouldn't you rather get to Fort Worth a day early and relax—after doing your gym routine, of course?"

"Honestly," LeAnn said, "I'm going stir-crazy all by myself. Dolly and Reba haven't been around much lately. Dolly's hitting up the corporate offices in each town, talking with both the WPRC's and the MPRC's marketing departments. It looks like they might hire her on full-time, if things with the bull riding go well."

"I've seen Reba hanging around the bulls."

LeAnn nodded. "She's made herself available as an on-call veterinarian at all of the rodeos, freelancing and filling in when needed. Both the WPRC and the MPRC have already made her an offer for full-time work, but for the moment, she's not sure that's what she wants to do. But all of that means that Reba and Dolly are pretty much out of the Winnebago except to sleep, so I've got it to myself more often than not. They're going to take the truck to Fort Worth. I'm trailering Garth to the RV and taking him."

"I'm going to have to spend the day at Hickory Livestock tomorrow. You'd probably be bored."

In other words, he didn't want her there. "Yeah, okay." LeAnn didn't want to feel rejected, but she did. She'd just have to coordinate her driving with her sisters or get an audio book to keep her occupied for the drive.

And Dylan was right—it would be good to relax a bit

before Dolly got her marketing plans underway. Still, she would have liked to have him with her. Maybe she'd hit the bars with the other women bull riders and hope that she didn't run into Mick.

"How's Lola doing?" she asked.

Dylan blew out a sigh. "I'm worried about her. I had Reba take a look at her and she says she's doing fine. But I know my horse. She's slowing down. I'm thinking of skipping out on the roping events, just to give her a break."

"That's too bad," she said. "I know how much Garth likes to compete and I think Lola feels the same way."

"She does. And Lord knows I could use the money from the prizes if we won. But I don't have the means to take care of her if she pushes it. Not to mention I don't know how I'd get another horse."

"You've been with her a long time?" Garth had been with her since the beginning, so she could understand where Dylan was coming from.

He nodded. "I bought her when I won my first all-around about seven years ago. Up until that, I had a few older horses, but we never bonded the way I've bonded with Lola."

"How did you get started with bull riding?"

"I couldn't afford a good horse," he said with a half-laugh. "The rodeo provided the bulls so all I had to do was hitch a ride to the next rodeo. But I rode some on my uncle's ranch, growing up."

"Did you ride in high school?"

"Yeah, when I could. My parents weren't supportive of the sport."

"Mine weren't either, at first. They wanted me to be a pageant queen, maybe follow in Dolly's footsteps and become a professional cheerleader."

"What made you pick rodeo?"

"It was more exciting, although the outfits are prettier in the pageants."

"I like you in jeans and a buttoned-down shirt," he said.

Pleasure flashed through her at the compliment and the appreciative gleam in his eyes.

"I liked you out of them too."

Now his smile turned deliciously devilish.

With her packed schedule and how hard she was going to have to work to come out on top in this event, LeAnn didn't have time for a boyfriend and all the nonsense that got crammed into a boyfriend-girlfriend relationship. But she'd love to have someone to hang out with and maybe kiss good night. Her gaze dropped to his lips. Her eyelids grew heavy as she remembered feeling them slide over her body. And other things.

"Are you falling asleep on me?" Dylan asked. "Because I was going to ask if you wanted to go to a matinee."

"I'd love that," she said.

"When are the bulls going to get to Fort Worth?" she asked as he settled the check.

"They should be there by tomorrow night." He looked up from signing the credit card slip. "Under no circumstances are you to get on one until I get there. I want to go over each of their strengths and weaknesses with you."

"I promise," she said, linking her arm through his as

they walked out of the restaurant. It almost felt like they were on a date.

"What movie do you want to see?" she asked.

"Something to take my mind off of things."

LeAnn suggested a new superhero movie and he agreed. "What's on your mind?" she asked.

"I don't want to talk about it."

"Okay." She'd let him get away with it for right now, but she intended to circle back later. When they got to the movie theater, she insisted on buying the tickets, which made him scowl.

"I invited you. It's only fair that I pay," Dylan said.

That was ridiculous. Even if they were dating, she didn't think that was a good way to do things. More often than not, Mick had been too broke to take her places so if she didn't pay for both of them, they wound up at a bar looking for fans to buy them drinks. If they had budgeted better, they could have gone to more places by splitting the costs.

"You can get the popcorn," she allowed. "Extra butter."

"We just had lunch."

"You can't go to the movies and not have popcorn, Dylan. Everyone knows that."

He shrugged, but bought two sodas as well.

While they were watching a superhero save the world, LeAnn enjoyed sitting next to him. If they had been dating, she would have leaned her head against his shoulder or encouraged him to put his arm around her so she could snuggle closer. She missed that intimacy. The best she could do was spread out in her seat so their arms and legs touched.

At the end of the movie, they still had half a bucket of popcorn left over, so they took it with them. He drove her back to where she had parked the Winnebago.

"Do you want to come in?" she asked. "I've got some board games we could play and then for dinner we could order pizza or I could grill some burgers."

"I appreciate the offer," he said, "but I've got a few things to do. I want to devote my day to the bulls tomorrow before getting on the road."

"I'm happy to help," she said, hoping she didn't sound desperate.

"Keep loose. Do some more stretches. If you get bored, hit the mechanicals."

"Right," she said, resisting a sigh. "I need to run Garth through some patterns anyway."

"I'll see you in Fort Worth," he said, turning to go.

"Wait." She caught his arm.

Dylan turned back to her with a puzzled expression on his face.

"Thanks for today." She stood up on her tiptoes and kissed him on the cheek.

Her lips tingled when they brushed against his scruff.

"Anytime, Killer," he said, warmly. For a moment, she thought he was going to kiss her, and her entire body thrilled at the expectation. But he pulled away reluctantly and got into his truck.

LeAnn watched him drive away, before blasting some music to clear out the melancholy that was creeping up on her. She wanted more days like this. More time with

Dylan. It didn't have to take over her life or get in the way of her training. She was going to have to figure out a way to make that happen, though, without ruining their friendship or mentorship. She hoped he wanted the same thing.

Chapter Twelve

JACKSON BLEVINS HAD made arrangements with the Fort Worth arena for them to practice. The arena owner, however, had sold tickets to allow some fans in to watch the women bull riders. Dylan wouldn't have minded it so much, but a lot of them were assholes who were there just to catcall and jeer at the women.

"We're used to it," Muriel said, when Dylan was about to go into the stands and throw a few of them out.

"Although, this is the worst I've seen it," LeAnn said, frowning at Muriel's hand on his arm.

"You shouldn't have to get used to it," he said between his teeth.

"Preach," Callie Brown said. She was a new addition to the group of women riders who had been invited to practice with them. This was her first and only event with the WPRC and she rode better than half the men did. LeAnn and the rest were going to have a hard time beating her. Callie had been riding bulls with her brothers on their farm since she was a child.

Still, LeAnn was learning a lot from her and the hollowness in Dylan's gut eased a little when no one got injured while they rode. The bulls were green, but they weren't docile and while he could have ridden one with his eyes closed, he was glad that they were the ones he'd suggested for the women.

Unfortunately, not everyone was happy about it.

"These bulls aren't going to be high scorers," LeAnn said, scowling into the pen after practice.

"I should get my daddy to send some real bulls over," Callie said.

"Talk to Jackson Blevins about it," Dylan said, refusing to get involved in the conversation. He had picked the twenty best bulls he saw from Mr. Blevins's stock. They weren't powerful enough to compete with the bulls that were already in the men's division, but they were solid and had potential. But most of all, Dylan was confident that these bulls would give the new riders a challenge, but would not turn deadly.

When everyone had cleaned up and put away the equipment, Dylan wasn't surprised that Muriel had decided to stick around to talk to him.

"What are you doing tonight?" she asked.

He had been hoping to convince LeAnn to go out to dinner with him, only he hadn't had a chance to talk to her about it. She had been gung-ho to ride the bulls this morning. They'd had just enough time for him to give her a rundown on all of them before the other riders arrived.

"I'm busy," Dylan said, trying to make a graceful escape.

"All night?" she asked, linking her arm through his.

"Muriel, I told you—I'm not interested in anything more than what we had."

"I get that," she said. "I'm not looking for a marriage proposal. I just want dinner and a good time tonight."

Before LeAnn, Dylan might have been tempted. But if there was anyone he wanted a good time with, it was LeAnn and not Muriel. "I'm not the one," he said.

"Whatever," she said, unlinking her arm. "I figured I'd give you first shot."

"I'm flattered."

"Save it. It's your loss."

"It is," he said, but was greatly relieved when she moved on to one of the bullfighters.

He was pleasantly surprised to see LeAnn leaning against her truck in the parking lot. At first, he was hoping that she was hanging around to talk to him, but then he noticed the scowl on her face.

"What?" he said.

"We're never going to beat the men's scores if we have to ride these weak-ass bulls," she said.

"You're not trying to beat their scores. You're competing against the other riders in the WPRC, not the MPRC."

"No one is going to want to watch us ride these bulls."

"Yes, they will. You'll see this weekend."

The WPRC was really building up the event. The eight women riders were doing a whole media tour next week. Dylan was a little pissed it was cutting into LeAnn's training time, but he was going to make sure she kept up with her weight training.

LeAnn still looked disgusted.

"Do you want to grab some dinner?" he asked.

She stared at him suspiciously. "If I get a steak and mac

and cheese, are you going to make me do extra cardio?"

"I promise I won't." He crossed his heart.

"All right then. You drive." She climbed into his truck.

He took her to a place outside of the normal area because he didn't want to run into anyone they knew—not that he gave a shit if anyone saw them together. Dylan just didn't want to share her with anyone.

As it was, a few people came up to them at the restaurant for pictures and autographs. Over dessert—a huge slice of cheesecake with strawberries smothering it—LeAnn wagged her fork at him. "Can I ask you a question?"

"Shoot."

"How come you didn't take Muriel up on her offer for dinner and a good time tonight?"

"You heard that, huh?"

"Mmmhmm," she said around a forkful of cheesecake.

"I didn't want to."

"Why not?"

She wasn't going to let it go, was she? "I'm just not that into her," he said, hoping she'd let the subject drop.

"You were into her before."

"That was before."

"Before what?"

Before you is what he wanted to say but couldn't. Instead, he decided to tell her what would hold him back from LeAnn if she wanted to get more serious. "I'm not boyfriend material."

"Why?" she asked again, spearing some strawberries. "You're not a horndog. You don't party all night. You're not a felon, a drunk or a drug addict. What's the deal?"

"That's your criteria for a good boyfriend? Not being one of those things? You need to up your standards."

"You didn't answer the question."

Feeling like he was on the spot, Dylan wished he had ordered something stronger than wine with his dinner. "I don't have a lot to offer a woman." Especially now.

"That's ridiculous," she said. "You're kind, sexy, and great in bed."

He blinked at her. Is that how she saw him? What about broke and never around? "Thank you, but I also don't have a lot of money. I live out of hotels when I win a rodeo event, and my truck when I don't. When money gets tight, and it comes down to feeding my horse or myself, I feed my horse."

"And you don't think that's special?" she said.

"I don't think any woman is looking for that in a guy."

"You were going to pay for dinner tonight, right?" LeAnn asked.

"Of course," he said, affronted. "I asked you out."

"And if you hadn't had the money, you wouldn't have asked me out, right?"

"Right."

"What if I asked you?"

Dylan hesitated, sensing a trap. "I'd offer to pay half, and if I didn't have half, I'd turn down the invitation."

"But you wouldn't let me know that was the reason you were turning me down."

"Right. I wouldn't want you to know that I was broke and I wouldn't want you to feel obligated to buy me dinner."

"Do you feel obligated to buy me dinner?" she asked innocently.

He narrowed his eyes at her. "That's different."

"No, it's not." She waggled her fork at him again. "The rules don't have to be different for men and women."

"Why do I think you're going to tie this back into bull riding?"

"Because I am."

"You realize that you're preaching to the choir here," he said.

"Not entirely. Is there a reason you think I couldn't ride a bull like Maniac or Implosion?"

Dylan shuddered. "Those bulls are a nightmare. There's no way I'd ever put a beginner rider on them."

"Okay," she said. "That's fair. But once I get enough training, is there a reason why I couldn't compete on a bull like Maniac?"

Dylan thought about it. "No. I mean there will always be risks because you weigh less than a full-grown man and your muscle and core strength are not as powerful."

"But that can be built up."

"Sure," he said, trying to find a reason that wouldn't sound like he was prejudiced against women riders.

"So eventually, you think that the WPRC could use the same bulls as the MPRC in their events."

"Possibly," he said, not willing to give her more than that. "There are too many variables for me to say for sure right now. But I see your point."

"Good. Then let's get back to your dating preferences."

"Why?" he said.

"Because I'd like to go out on dates with you."

That shocked the hell out of him. "I thought you didn't want to be distracted from training."

"I don't. But it doesn't have to be a distraction. Not if we don't let it. Look—" LeAnn said. "I'm a little lonely. I'd like someone to watch movies and go out to dinner with, like we have been doing."

"So as friends?" he asked, not sure where this was heading.

"I miss being held and touched," she said. "We're great in bed together, but I meant what I said about not being into casual sex. It's not casual for me. Does that scare you?"

"A bit," he said. "But honestly, not as much as I thought it would. Still, I've got nothing to offer you." He linked his fingers through hers.

"You're underestimating yourself," she said.

"Or you're overestimating me."

"I'm not looking for a wedding ring," she said. "That was my mistake with Mick and I'm not going to make it with you."

"I'm not Mick. If you want to wait until marriage before having sex, I respect that."

"I'd be a little hypocritical to want that now."

"Bullshit," he said more forcefully than he intended. He modified his tone when she jumped. "You can do whatever you want."

"I didn't want to have sex with Mick. But I really like having sex with you."

Fire shot through every inch of Dylan's body. "Should I get the check?" he asked.

"Not just yet," she said. "I want to make sure we're on the same page."

"What do you want from this? From me?" he asked, willing to give her just about anything.

"I want to be with you. I want to matter to you."

"I want that too," he said, the breath catching in his throat. "And you do matter to me. That's why I can see that you could do so much better than me."

"And I could do so much worse. Hell, I've had worse. I need to train hard, but I'm realizing now that I also need to have something other than rodeo in my life."

"And you think that something could be me?"

"I hope so. If you feel the same way."

"I'm not sure what I feel, only that I do want to be with you." *I just don't want to be a disappointment.* "I don't want whatever this is between us to get in the way of training." *I don't want to miss something that could put you in danger, like I might have done with Johnny.*

Shaking her head, LeAnn said, "I won't let it. I need to beat Callie. I have to stay focused on improving. When I was with Mick, I wasn't allowed to do that. I was always worried about keeping him happy. I felt that because I wasn't sleeping with him, I had to make up for it by being the world's best girlfriend in other areas."

"I don't want you to feel like you're obligated to sleep with me," he said.

"Good, because I don't."

"Damn straight." He clinked glasses with her.

"Still, I don't want you to feel pressured about being in a relationship with me. I just want to have fun."

"I can do that."

"That's a relief. I thought I'd have to hog-tie you to get you to realize that I wasn't trying to get you to the altar. There is one thing, though," LeAnn said.

Here it comes, Dylan thought. This was the other boot he'd been waiting for her to drop.

"If you want to have sex with someone else, you've got to tell me first. I don't want to catch you and Muriel—or whoever—doing the nasty."

"I'm not Mick," he said.

"If you were, I wouldn't even be here right now," she said solemnly.

"I would never do that to you."

"Good."

Part of him wanted to wait until he had the horse rescue ranch or at the very least a home base, but he realized that he was tired of waiting for good things in his life. He wanted her and for some reason, she wanted him. "I just don't want to break your heart if things don't work out."

"I don't want to break your heart either," she countered.

"You really are a pain in the ass—you know that?" he said, with grudging admiration.

"Thank you. Now, you can pay the bill this time. I'm getting it next time, though."

He opened his mouth to argue.

"No," she said, stuffing a forkful of cheesecake into his mouth. "And if either one of us is too stretched until the next rodeo, we do something that doesn't cost a lot of money."

It sounded too good to be true. He'd get to know her better and they could spend more time together. She knew not to expect much from him so the chance that he'd let her down was reduced.

"You can trust me, LeAnn," he said after he swallowed the cheesecake. "I'll never pressure you to do anything you don't want to."

She covered her hand with his. "And I'll never pressure you to do anything you don't want to." LeAnn dug around in her purse and pulled out a pen and a scrap of paper.

"What are you doing?" he asked.

"We're going to set down some rules and guidelines, so you don't have to worry about anything."

"Sweetheart, I'm not worried."

"Well, then let's just call this managing expectations. We've already talked about sex. We're mutually exclusive. That's a hard rule."

"Agreed," he said, watching as she wrote that down with her chicken-scratch handwriting.

"Two… We should share at least one meal a day together unless we're busy or in another state."

He nodded. "That seems reasonable."

She looked up at him. "I don't think it's any of our parents' business if we're dating, but I'm not going to keep it a secret. I'm done with lying and hiding things."

"I don't speak with my parents that often," he said. "But I might have to in the next few weeks if things don't pan out for me. They'll probably want to see me in person. Do you want to come with me?"

"Yes, please," she said. "I'd love to meet your parents."

"Don't get your hopes up. They're not like your parents."

"That might be a good thing," she said.

"I disagree, but I suppose the grass always looks greener on the other side. They were pretty much the exact opposite of your parents in every way. They were happy to foist me off on my uncle."

"Why?"

Dylan played with his straw in his drink. "I had a brother who died when he was sixteen."

Placing a hand over her heart, LeAnn gasped. "I'm so sorry."

"His name was Danny. He was six years older than me, and I idolized him. But after he died, my parents just checked out. He crashed his new car. The cops said he had been going too fast around a corner and just lost control of it."

"That's awful."

Nodding, Dylan reached over to hold her hand. "Sometimes I think they lost both of us that day. After that, it was like I couldn't do anything right. And then, when I started getting into rodeo, they shipped me off to my uncle's ranch. I barely saw them after that."

"What about now?" she asked. "Did being away make things any easier in the long run?"

"It was easier for me to do what I wanted. But we don't have much of a relationship."

"Then why would you go and see them?"

Dylan pointed to her list. "I've got to add one. Always be honest with each other."

She nodded vigorously and wrote it down. "Definitely."

"Okay in the interest of complete honesty, the reason I'm considering seeing my parents again is because I'm flat broke. I might have to swallow my pride and ask them for a loan."

"For what?"

"There's a farm that I've had my eye on. It's going up for auction in a few weeks. The banks turned my loan applications down."

Staring at him, LeAnn tapped the pen on the table in thought. "What are you going to do with the farm?"

"I'm going to start a horse rescue. Take in unwanted horses and board the older ones for owners who don't want to get rid of them, but don't have a place for them."

"I think that's wonderful," she said.

"It will be if I can get the money for the down payment. My business plan is solid."

"Can I see it?"

"Sure," he said, flattered. "It's pretty boring reading."

"Not to me."

If she kept looking at him like he'd hung the moon in the sky, he was going to fall in love with her, if he wasn't already halfway there.

"Will you and Lola be retiring when that happens?"

"I'm not sure. But yeah, probably. I'm hitting the end of my bull-riding time. I want to get out while I'm still healthy and with a few wins."

LeAnn nodded, her eyes far away. "Will you still coach?"

Cupping her cheek until she looked at him, he said, "I'll be here as long as you need me."

"Good," she said. "Because I want to continue training with you for the rest of the season."

He let his hand drop. "You're not saying that because I just told you I was broke and need the money, are you?"

"No, I'm saying that because Callie is better than me and you'll give me an edge."

They exchanged challenging stares for a moment. In the end, he believed her. "Okay, you've got me. Both as a coach and a..."

"Boyfriend," LeAnn said.

Dylan winced. "Really?"

"Say it."

"It sounds so high school-ish."

"I suppose I could call you bae."

"Boyfriend it is," he said. "And I'm proud to be your man."

"I like the sound of that," LeAnn said, breathless. Getting up from the booth, she shimmied in next to him on the other side. "Now we need to kiss to seal the deal."

"Do we?" he said, dipping his head to hers. "Oh well, if I must."

The kiss was sweet and too short, but he was amused that LeAnn didn't let herself get distracted. "Let's talk about the bulls I'm going to ride tomorrow."

Chapter Thirteen

Fort Worth, TX—May

SHE DIDN'T GO eight seconds. Not once during the exhibition. On her last ride, she hit the ground hard, gasping for air. The whole crowd was silent as they waited to see if she would get up. Finally, she staggered to her feet, humiliated but unhurt.

Dylan approached her after she got out of the arena, his eyes filled with concern. She must look as dejected as she felt. "Are you okay?" he asked softly.

LeAnn shook her head wearily. "I don't know," she admitted. "I thought I was getting better, but I guess not."

Dylan put an arm around her shoulders comfortingly. "It's okay," he said gently. "You'll go eight seconds next time."

LeAnn wanted to believe him, but she wasn't sure if she could face another failure in front of all these people, in front of the other athletes. She leaned into the hug, glad that she was entitled to it now that they were official. Dylan steered her into the equipment shed so that they were away from prying eyes.

She clung to him, burying her face into his soft cotton shirt. His spicy aftershave tickled her nose and the slow circles he was rubbing on her lower back soothed some of the pain.

"This is nice," she muttered, content to be held.

"I know you don't believe me, but you're improving."

Giving an unladylike snort, LeAnn said, "Callie went the full eight seconds. So did Muriel and Kim."

"So will you," he said. "You'll do it when it counts."

"Are you sure about that?" she asked, raising her head.

"Positive." He smiled down at her.

"Thank you," she said, closing her eyes.

"For what?"

"It was getting to me. Not meeting the crowd's expectations. Not meeting my parents' expectations. But most of all, falling short of my own goals. You have a way of making me feel better, just by being here."

"Glad to help." He brushed a kiss on her nose.

She leaned up and kissed him before he could get too far away. Wrapping her arms around his neck, she let her mouth slowly move over his. Dylan held her close, and she loved how her body fit against his. Moving restlessly against him, she wished they were back in the RV or in a hotel room. But before it could get too heated and she gave in to the temptation to start unbuckling and unbuttoning, she reluctantly broke off the kiss.

"Damn, that was nice," he said, rubbing his thumb over her puffy lower lip.

She wanted to bite it in frustration, but she behaved herself. They could play around a bit after the rodeo. Right now, she had another event to compete in. And this one, she would win.

"I'm going to get ready for barrel racing," LeAnn said reluctantly stepping away from him.

"Okay," he said. "I'll see you after." Dylan pulled her in for another quick hug. "Go get 'em, Killer." He stayed with the bulls while she made her way to the other side of the rodeo.

Stiff and feeling bruised, LeAnn went over what had gone wrong in her rides. At least her scores—or non-scores in this case—wouldn't count against her yet. She hated disappointing the rodeo fans. She also hated that the bulls she had called weak and boring were kicking her ass so hard.

Because she was focused on doing better, she didn't notice that Mick had caught up to her.

"What do you want?" she groaned. She was not in the mood to hear him bitch about women bull riders.

"Can't an old friend say hello?"

"We're not friends," LeAnn said.

"Well, that hurts." Mick held a hand over his heart and tried to look charming.

It might have worked except she knew how full of shit he really was. "I need to get Garth, so I can't talk."

"I hear that you've been asking questions about Dylan Porter," Mick said.

Well, she had been. But only to the other women riders and mostly about why he didn't have a girlfriend. Mick was a little late with that type of information.

"I don't think you'll want him to coach you when you hear what I have to tell you."

He thought it was about coaching. LeAnn smirked.

"I've already hired him to train me for the rest of the season."

Mick stepped in front of her, and she had to stop in her tracks or run right into him. "I was afraid of that. You've got to hear me out."

"Fine," she sighed out, annoyed. Anything to get him to go away.

"Do you remember Johnny Montana?"

"Yeah," LeAnn said. "He died last season after he wrecked. The bull stomped on him before the bullfighters got him clear." She hadn't watched the event, but Dolly had told her about it. "Sad. I feel for his family."

"Well, you should talk to his parents."

"I don't want to talk to anyone's parents. Least of all grieving ones." Then her conscience twinged at her. "Unless you think I could help somehow."

"They would tell you that Dylan Porter was their son's bull-riding coach."

"That's awful," she cried. Dylan must have been devastated.

"He's a bad teacher," Mick said, placing a hand on her arm. She shook it off. "I just don't want you to get shitty advice or worse and wind up getting hurt because of his negligence."

LeAnn didn't know what angle Mick was going for, but she wasn't going to let him put a wedge between her and Dylan. "I know what I'm doing. And I trust Dylan."

"Do you?" Mick asked. "Or are you looking for a father figure now that your dad's gone home, and you see one in Dylan?"

"Ew," she said. "Dylan is only a few years older than us."

"Really?" Mick said, cocking his head in puzzlement. "Because he acts like an old fart. I just assumed he was getting too old to bull ride and was looking to stay relevant by coaching."

"That's not the case." LeAnn sidestepped him and continued toward the barn.

Mick kept pace with her. "I would be glad to help you get better at riding bulls."

Go to hell. "No thanks," she said instead.

"LeAnn, I'm worried about you."

"Don't be," she called over her shoulder. At least he had stopped following her. His words bothered her, though, but more because she knew Dylan would be mourning his friend. Dolly wouldn't have recommended Dylan if she hadn't thought he was a good trainer. And Dolly would have known that he had been training Johnny Montana. She wouldn't have suggested Dylan if she thought he'd put her in danger. LeAnn would talk to him about it tonight and make sure he knew that she believed in him.

She was surprised to see Merry and Dolly chatting by the barrel-racing section.

"Got time for a beer tonight?" LeAnn asked Merry when she came up to them.

"Always," Merry said. "Dolly and I were talking about the sponsors you were looking to get."

"Yeah," LeAnn said. "Lila Rogers with Cowboy Couture."

"She's a tough nut to crack," Dolly said. "I think it would be a better choice to go with Sierra Boots."

Merry made a face. "Like I was saying, Dolly, Sierra Broadway has very high standards for the athletes Sierra Boots decides to sponsor. No drinking is number one on their list."

"LeAnn can do that," Dolly said.

LeAnn looked at her sister. "How much are they paying for that?"

"Enough that you can drink at home instead of the bars."

"No public displays of affection," Merry ticked off on her fingers.

"That's okay," Dolly said. "LeAnn doesn't have a boyfriend."

"Actually," LeAnn said. "Dylan and I are seeing each other."

"What?" Dolly did a double take.

"Good for you. He's a hottie," Merry said.

"Why didn't you tell me about this?" Dolly looked hurt.

"It all happened rather quickly," she said. "I'll give you the details later."

"Over a soda instead of a beer," Merry said. "Unless you want to cross Sierra Boots off the list."

"I don't think we can," Dolly said. "They've expressed interest in you."

This is what they had wanted. "Okay," LeAnn said reluctantly. "Merry, can you come by the Winnebago for that beer?"

"Look," Merry said. "I know how hard it is to get a sponsor. And how having that money is nice to have so you're not relying on winning a fat purse every rodeo. But you don't want to change who you are for the sponsor opportunity. It just isn't worth it."

Yeah, but who was she? She wasn't Little Miss Goody-Two-Shoes and she wasn't a Wild Grayson Sister. Just where did she fit in? LeAnn would have to level up her game. And bull riding was where she was going to shine. She had four more months, four states and less than twenty events to make it happen.

"Having Sierra Boots backing me will get me through the season," LeAnn said. "I can manage not to drink or kiss Dylan in public."

Merry shrugged. "It's your call. But I think you should still pursue Lila Rogers. Cowboy Couture doesn't have so many restrictions."

"I'm not giving up on trying to attract them," Dolly said.

"Me neither," LeAnn said.

"Well, I've got to get back to the announcer's booth. We'll get that beer sooner or later."

"Thanks for everything, Merry," LeAnn said, glad to have her advice.

"Also," Merry said as she turned to go. "Watch out for Debbi Peterson," Merry said. "Not only is she riding well today, but she's also been talking shit about you. Stupid stuff, but if Sierra Boots gets wind of it, it could sabotage an offer."

"This isn't about Mick, is it?" LeAnn rolled her eyes.

"Because he's been schmoozing up on me lately and I am so not interested."

"She's jealous," Dolly said. "It's because the WPRC and the MPRC want to push you and Mick as the new faces of the organization."

"Gross," LeAnn said.

"Gross, but good for attracting sponsors. I'm not saying you have to be nice to the son of a bitch, just smile for the cameras."

"And don't turn your back on Debbi. She's a two-faced little snake," Merry said.

"Thanks for the warning."

It had been easier when it was only about the riding, but LeAnn figured this was part of leveling up. She tried to force all that to the back of her mind. She had to concentrate on barrel racing right now. And if she could make Debbi Peterson eat her dust, that would be a bonus.

Chapter Fourteen

DYLAN'S BODY WAS still humming from the heat of LeAnn's kisses this morning, but the sensation quickly faded as he filled out his reports on the bulls for Mr. Hickory on a brand-new tablet that he barely understood how to use. He saw that LeAnn's sister, Reba, was also in the pens with the bulls and he walked up to her as she was examining an animal named Terminal.

"Is everything okay?" he asked.

"Just doing a routine pre-ride exam," she said. She shied away from him and gave him a nervous look. Dylan wasn't sure why Reba seemed skittish around him, but he read her body language and backed off a few steps.

"Are you working for Mr. Hickory too?" He wondered if she was still upset with him for "letting" LeAnn ride the bull in the rodeo's season opener.

"No, the WPRC hired me for the next few rodeos to collect data on the bulls." Her face smoothed over as she took another step away from him. It seemed she was more comfortable with him at a distance. Dylan tried not to take it personally.

"What type of data?" he asked.

"We're looking to compare the stock between all of the

breeders. I'll be running tests on your uncle's bulls too."

"So the WPRC is looking to get bulls from breeders other than Hickory Livestock?"

Reba shrugged. "I'm not a part of those decisions. But why put all your eggs in one basket?"

That made sense and his uncle would be pleased to hear it.

"We also want to see if they're the right type of animal athletes we're looking for."

"Mr. Hickory wouldn't offer substandard bulls," Dylan said.

"No one is suggesting he is," Reba said. "But with any new event or challenge, it's good to have all the data and see if there are ways of cutting costs without sacrificing quality. Or on the other hand, if it's worth it to invest in stock that has higher potential."

That didn't sound good. It sounded to him like the WPRC was looking for wilder bulls. "Do you need any help?"

"No thank you," she said politely, typing something into her own tablet.

Leaving her to do her job, Dylan continued on with his reports. When it was time for him to get Lola prepped for their tie-down roping event, he tossed his tablet into the glove compartment of his truck and spent a few minutes stretching. After gathering up his gear, he went to the barn to collect Lola.

After saddling her up and riding her over to the roping arena, something felt off to him, but Dylan couldn't put his finger on it. They lined up by the pen with the other single-rider ropers. The group roping was just finishing up and the crowd was worked up.

The first prize was seven thousand, six hundred dollars and Dylan wanted that purse.

Getting his rope prepared, Dylan noticed that Lola was dancing around more than normal. He chalked that up to excess energy. When it was their turn in the start area, Dylan secured the rope that was going to tie the calf's legs between his teeth. The other lasso was in his hands, ready to loop around the calf's head. When the calf's gate opened, Lola broke through the tape while Dylan twirled the rope over his head. The calf was fast, but he roped him around the neck on his first toss. Leaping off of Lola, Dylan followed the rope down to the calf. Picking up the calf, he turned him on his back and secured the legs—6.86.

With a big grin, Dylan leapt back on top of Lola in victory—and felt her leg buckle.

Shit.

He jumped back off and led her out of the arena. He didn't even think about the cheering crowd or his number-one score.

"I need a vet," he said to one of the crew. "Get me Reba Keller. She's by the bulls."

BY THE TIME that Reba was finished with her examination of Lola, Dylan was a nervous wreck. He was only vaguely aware that he had won the $7,600.00. Good. He was going to need it for vet bills.

"How is she?" he asked, when Reba came out of the stall with the portable ultrasound machine the WPRC owned.

"She's fine," Reba said, patting the horse's neck affectionately. "I've started her on cold therapy and wrapped the leg to reduce swelling. Tonight, you should rub on some anti-inflammatories. Keep her in the stall until it's time to put her in the trailer."

"Thanks," he said, rubbing a hand over his face.

"Hey," she said, putting a hand on his arm. "Do you want me to go get LeAnn?"

He looked up in surprise. This was a different Reba than the one who had been outside checking out the bulls. She seemed more at ease and less intimidated by him. Maybe because she was in her element here. Maybe because she sensed he was worried about Lola and she was trying to comfort him. "No," Dylan said. "I'll talk to her later."

"Okay. She has my number, if Lola needs me."

"I appreciate it."

"Not a problem."

After Reba left, it was all Dylan could do not to sink to the ground in defeat. He had to find a place that he trusted to take care of Lola before she suffered a more serious injury. He needed a new horse fast, if he wanted to keep competing. That meant quick cash.

He had the win from the roping today, but he'd need almost double to get a trained rodeo horse to replace Lola. The only way he could see doing that was getting a bigger sponsorship. His next call was to Dolly Keller.

"Do you still need cowboys for that shirtless calendar?"

he asked, hoping that his mother wouldn't see it.

"Sorry, I'm all booked for next year's calendar. But I'll put you on the list for the year after."

Dylan didn't know whether to be disappointed or relieved. It still left him in a bind moneywise, but he got to keep his dignity.

"Can I ask why you're suddenly interested?"

Great. He was going to have to admit to LeAnn's sister how broke he was. Way to make a good impression. Deciding not to answer directly, he said, "How about sponsorships? I know you're working on getting a few for LeAnn. Were there any that were looking for someone like me?" Even before the words were out of his mouth, he knew that the answer was going to be no. But Dolly surprised him.

"We-eell," she drawled out. "I could try and spin you and LeAnn as the next 'it' couple of the rodeo."

"Really?" he said, wincing. That was almost as bad as the shirtless calendar. He didn't like everyone in his business. "I don't think LeAnn would go for it."

"She will," Dolly assured him. "Better you than Mick."

"Wait, what?" What the hell did that asshole Mick have anything to do with?

"Don't worry about it. Let me put something together and get back to you guys. It would help if you have a really big win in San Antonio next week."

Dylan looked down at his phone and fiddled with it until San Antonio's bull roster came up. Each rodeo, the bull riders chose five bulls that they were willing to ride. The names went into a drawing and were assigned to the riders. Sometimes you got your first choice, sometimes your last. And sometimes, you were the only one who wanted a bull.

One bull remained unchosen this round. Fever Dream was a son of a bitch. He should know. He was one of his uncle's best bulls. No one wanted to ride that damn beast. He had never held a rider on his back for eight seconds. Many cowboys had tried him, Dylan included. All of them had landed on their ass or worse within a few seconds. Fever Dream would be a high-scoring bull...if Dylan could stay on.

It would send his ranking into the stratosphere and maybe even attract a sponsor that Dolly could hook him up with.

"Tell them to watch me this Sunday. I'm going to win by riding a bull named Fever Dream. He has a one-hundred-percent career buck-off."

"Impressive. If you can do it, it'll make my job a lot easier," Dolly said. "We'll talk about this later."

After she hung up, Dylan wondered just what he'd gotten himself into. Shaking his head, he went over to where his uncle's bulls were being penned. Sure enough, Fever Dream was giving anyone who came close to the fence a menacing bump. He was a white bull, heavily muscled with black spots on his flanks. Lunging at him, Fever Dream crashed into the metal fence and pawed at the ground.

"I'm coming for you," Dylan said to him, but Fever Dream didn't seem too worried.

He watched the bull pace back and forth and remembered their rides. This bull was not going to make it easy for him. Dylan would have to review some of the other riders' experiences and see if he could come up with a strategy. But right now, he needed to finish assessing Hickory Livestock's bulls for the women riders in San Antonio.

When he called in the results to Mr. Hickory, Dylan told him that he was planning on riding Fever Dream next week.

"You're going to have crappy odds," Mr. Hickory said thoughtfully.

"That's why I'm going to surprise a lot of people when I win."

"You sound confident."

Dylan had to be, because if he allowed a moment of doubt, it would eat away at him. "He's my uncle's bull. I'm familiar with his tricks." Sure, he'd been thrown every time he had been on him, both on and off the circuit, but Dylan had the bull's number now. He could beat him.

"Then, I'm going to put some money on you."

Dylan resisted the urge to groan. Great, now his boss's money was on the line. "I hope I make bank for you."

"How's Killer coming along? Should I place a bet on her too?"

Dylan sucked in a breath. "No. Not yet."

"The money is good on her to win since she's had such a poor showing."

"She's doing just fine." Dylan felt the need to defend her.

"If I wait until she goes eight seconds, the odds won't be as sweet."

"You shouldn't risk the money on anything but a sure thing."

"And you're a sure thing?" Mr. Hickory said.

Refusing to hesitate, Dylan said, "I am."

"I think I'm going to place a bet on Killer Keller anyway to win. I'd appreciate you doing everything in your power to make that happen."

"I'll see what I can do." Dylan had no idea what the heck he could do that he wasn't already doing. But for San Antonio, he needed to concentrate on how he was going to stay on Fever Dream.

Chapter Fifteen

San Antonio, TX—June

IT HAD BEEN a rough few days. She and Dylan had barely seen each other this week. LeAnn had had to do a ton of press circuits and attend sponsorship events while keeping up with her training. The good news was she was getting experience riding all of the bulls in the Hickory Livestock pens. The bad news was her back was killing her and she was bruised and sore. When Dylan wasn't training her, he was researching and practicing to ride Fever Dream in his event. No one had ever stayed on Fever Dream long enough to score, but if anyone could do it, it was Dylan.

But she was worried about him. He was working himself too hard, whether it was out of guilt for still riding Lola or something else, she didn't know. She hoped it wasn't about taking their relationship to the next level, but she wondered if he'd felt forced into it. If she had stayed out of his bed, Dylan would have one less complication in his life.

A sliver of guilt was starting to distract her, and she had to forcibly keep her mind on the bulls. LeAnn had wanted to talk to Dylan about Johnny Montana too, but she didn't want to distract him with bad thoughts or energy before the ride.

"I've got an idea," LeAnn said while they were both waiting to practice on their respective bulls.

"What's that?" he asked.

She didn't like the dark circles under his eyes or the lines by his mouth. It was obvious that he wasn't getting enough sleep.

"Not too far away from here is the Three Sisters Ranch in Last Stand. Why don't we take a drive, and you can board Lola there for a little while? Just to give her the R&R that she deserves."

"That's Trent Campbell's ranch, right?"

"His wife and her sisters own it, but yeah, that's where his school is located."

"Is it a good place?" he asked.

"Definitely. They love horses there. And they have a good vet who's local."

"I'll have to call them up and see how much it's going to cost me," he said tiredly.

"I already asked. It's going to be about $500 a month, but if you prepay, they'll give you a twenty-percent discount."

"It'll depend on how well I do this weekend," he said. "But I think I can swing one month, if you want to head there tonight."

"I'd like that," LeAnn said.

"All right. Let's grab dinner on the road and head over there once they kick us out tonight."

"Okay," she said, glad to be able to spend some time with him. It was about a forty-five-minute drive to the Three Sisters Ranch, but maybe afterwards, he could hang out at her place until her sisters got home. She wouldn't mind if he stayed the night, but Dolly and Reba might find it uncomfortable to wake up and find Dylan there.

As she walked back to the arena, LeAnn couldn't stop worrying about Dylan's upcoming ride. Fever Dream was going to hurt Dylan—she just knew it. A part of her knew she sounded hypocritical, but she wished that Dylan had chosen a less dangerous bull to ride.

The excitement around the pens was almost tangible. A few of the cowboys were betting that Dylan would get knocked on his ass as soon as the bull left the chute. When Mick and his friends arrived at the pens, LeAnn circled around to join Muriel and Callie. Sure, it felt like she was running away, but she didn't want to deal with the men's stupidity right now.

"That bull is a demon," Callie said.

"Well, if anyone's going to ride him, it'll be Dylan," LeAnn said.

"What's the deal between you two, anyway?" Muriel asked.

LeAnn could lie, or she could just say the obvious—that he was her coach. But she wasn't going to do that anymore. She had nothing to be ashamed of, and nothing to be worried about. If her parents found out about Dylan through gossip, then she'd address that with them when the time came.

"You know he's my coach," LeAnn said. "Are you asking if we're dating?"

Muriel set her jaw. "Dylan doesn't date."

"He does now," LeAnn said.

"Damn," Callie said and gave a low whistle.

"He'll break your heart," Muriel said. LeAnn thought for a moment that Muriel was going to shove her or something.

"It's not like that," LeAnn said. "We're taking it slow. It's casual."

Muriel relaxed slightly at that. "Oh, you're talking *dating*, like you go out to movies and dinner."

"It's not your business if we're fucking or not," LeAnn said.

Callie snorted. "You kiss your mama with that mouth?"

"Not lately," Muriel said. "Mommy and Daddy went home, and it looks like little LeAnn is pretending to be all grown up."

"Muriel, don't be a bitch," Samantha, one of the other bull riders, said as she came up to them and leaned against the fence. "We've got enough crap to deal with today." She pointed her chin over at the male bull riders who were taking turns staring at them while Dylan was getting settled on top of his bull.

"Sam's right. We don't have to be BFFs," Callie said. "But we shouldn't make it easy for those guys to divide us."

"Especially over a man," Samantha said. "Muriel, you can have your pick of any of the riders over there. You only want Dylan because he said no after the first time." Samantha slapped her hand over her forehead. "Shit, LeAnn, I'm sorry. Did you know that he and Muriel got it on once?"

"Yeah," LeAnn said. "Dylan and I are honest with each other. I insisted on it after the fiasco with Mick."

"Mick's a dick," Muriel said.

There was a general agreement about that statement.

"Why is he still chasing me?" LeAnn grumbled.

"Because you're the one that got away," Samantha said.

"He wants to be your first," Muriel said in a singsong voice.

"Oh for fuck's sake," LeAnn said. "I'm not a virgin." She hadn't meant to blurt that out, but at the surprised looks on their faces, she was glad she had. "And it's none of your damned business who was my first, but I'll assure you it wasn't any asshole rodeo cowboy."

"That sly son of a bitch," Muriel said, pushing away from the fence and storming off.

"I supposed if we had to guess…" Callie said, looking over at Dylan.

Then the chute opened and all hell broke loose.

DYLAN HAD BEEN on wild bulls before. He'd ridden roller coasters. He had even jumped out of a plane once. But as soon as Fever Dream launched himself out of the chute, Dylan knew he was in trouble. It was like sitting on the back of a rocket. This bull was airborne and doing spins before his back hooves cleared the chute. Fever Dream did not like having a rider and seemed to feed on the frenzy of the crowd by whipping, bucking, and rolling. Dylan's neck nearly came off his shoulders. His hand almost came down and touched the bull—which would have disqualified him—but he managed to resist. He was about to come out of the saddle and go flying when he heard the eight-second buzzer. Holy shit, he'd done it.

Then he was airborne...only he wasn't far enough away from the bull. Fever Dream's hooves kicked him in the chest, and he felt the impact hard through his padded vest. The force pushed him back and he rolled a few feet. The ground shook as the bull leaped and twisted toward him, landing scant inches from his head.

"Move your ass," the bullfighter said, grabbing the bull's horn and twisting its head away from Dylan. Staggering to his feet, Dylan collapsed to his knees before pushing himself up again. Two bullfighters half carried, half dragged him to safety.

"Helluva ride," one of them said.

"You all right?" the other said. "Do you want a doctor?"

"I don't know yet," Dylan said, attempting to straighten away from them once the bull had returned to the corral. He waved to the roaring crowd. Both he and the bull had given them a good show. He should win this. And if he did, Lola was safe. He could afford to board her for a few months with this event's purse.

He spit blood onto the arena floor.

That wasn't good.

But when he looked up at the scoreboard, it made it all worthwhile. He was number one on the leaderboard with 175 points. The other riders would have to score over ninety points to catch up to him. Not impossible, but not likely either.

Grimacing at the taste of blood in his mouth, he moved away from the bucking chutes toward the backstage area.

He saw Dolly tottering over to him with a microphone and camera crew. But seeing the two people behind her was what made him stop dead in his tracks.

What the heck?

His mother stared at him with horrified eyes and his father scowled at him.

Great. Just what he needed in front of a live feed.

"Dylan, you did it. You rode the unrideable bull. What have you got to say to your fans?" Dolly shoved the microphone into his face.

"I hope I gave them a good show." It was second nature to want to push by them and go back into the locker room area so he could take off his gear and grab something to drink. But he forced himself to stay put. Dolly must have had a reason for ambushing him like this.

"Oh you certainly did. That was one hell of a kick you took as well."

"It was just a graze," he lied.

"Now, you and this bull have a history, don't you?" Dolly said, coming alongside of him. The cameraman stepped to follow. In a few seconds, his parents would be in the shot. Oh hell no. He would have moved, but Dolly gripped his arm like a vice and shot him a warning look.

"You could say that," Dylan gritted out. "My uncle owns Fever Dream."

"He's thrown you and every other rider in the past. Why was today so different?"

"It was just his time."

"Maybe it was your time too. Could it have been because your parents were in the audience?"

The cameraman swung to catch his parents in the shot.

"I didn't know they'd be here today," Dylan said in what he hoped was a mild tone.

"Lou told us you were riding Fever Dream today," his mother said.

"We were going to try and talk you out of it, but we were too late," his father said.

Suddenly, Dylan felt a lot like LeAnn. "I'm glad you were." He was a professional, damn it. He knew the dangers and his limits.

"We're glad you weren't hurt." Then, his mother launched herself at him and squeezed him hard.

His ribs protested and his knees buckled, but he managed to keep his gasp of pain inside and straightened up. Oh holy hell, that hurt. He was going to pay for this later, but he smiled for the camera, and patted his mother's back awkwardly.

"That's what we're all about here at the Men's Professional Rodeo Circuit of America—family and exceeding expectations. Next up, more rough-stock events. And cut." Dolly motioned with her hand and the cameraman stopped filming. "Thanks, guys. I appreciate the segment. Dylan, Sierra Boots is going to eat this up."

"Excuse me for a second," Dylan said, gently extracting himself from his mother and following Dolly out of the backstage area. "What are we looking at Sierra Boots for?"

"I'm going to shoot for a $50,000-dollar-a-year contract."

Dylan blinked. Hot damn.

"Minus fifteen percent for me. You'll need to put their

logo on your trailer and gear, though."

"Can do," he said.

"And there's some behavior rules that they're going to want you and LeAnn to abide by."

"What type of rules?" He frowned.

"Don't worry about that now. Let's wait and see the contract first. Go enjoy some time with your parents. I'll be in touch when I hear back from them. They may want to meet you in Oklahoma—that's where their headquarters are—so keep your schedule open."

"Okay," Dylan said. He wanted to keep walking with her, but he knew he had to go back and talk to his parents.

When he returned, his uncle had joined him.

"I'm glad it was you," Lou said, shaking his hand. "But I wouldn't have shed tears if you had wrecked."

"Thanks," Dylan said dryly.

"Are you really all right?" his mother said.

"I've been doing this almost half my life, Mom," he said in an even tone. But he couldn't resist adding, "Guess all those summers at Uncle Lou's paid off." Did he keep the bitterness out of his voice? He wasn't sure. But his mother seemed comforted by his words, which was odd.

"That's good." She gripped his father's arm. "I'm glad I listened to you all those years ago."

"Wait," Dylan said. "What's this now?"

"After Danny died, I wanted to keep you close," she said.

"Smother you," his father added.

"And you were so hell-bent on doing everything dangerous. When you wanted to do the rodeo events in high school, I panicked. We sent you off to Lou's so you'd either decide it was too much work to be a cowboy..."

"Or you'd get trained like a professional," his father said.

Lou puffed up with pride. "I think we can all see what happened."

That wasn't how Dylan remembered it. "I thought you were glad to get rid of me."

"No," his mother said, shaking her head. "It was hard to be away from you after we lost Danny. It was all I could do not to go out there every weekend and call every night to check up on you," his mother added.

His father nodded. "We just wanted you to be safe and happy," he said.

Dylan realized that aside from seeing the way his uncle treated the old farm animals, he had been happy. And all that hard work had helped him work through his feelings about Danny's death. Looking back, he could now see it through his parents' eyes. Grief made everyone do crazy things. Johnny Montana's father shot the bull that had thrown his son to his death. Dylan's father had sacrificed seeing him daily to gain peace of mind that he'd be safe in the rodeo. This was a lot to unpack. Dylan was left feeling like his world had just taken a giant tilt.

"You gave us a scare today," his mother said.

"But we wanted to let you know that we're awfully proud of you." His father nodded.

Had Fever Dream kicked him in the head instead of the chest? Dylan didn't think he'd ever hear his father say those words to him.

Clearing his throat because it was clogged with emotion, Dylan said, "Thank you."

"Why don't we all have dinner together after the rodeo?" Lou suggested. "We can catch up and Dylan can tell you all about his plans to open up a ranch for retired rodeo horses."

His father looked interested, and Dylan wasn't sure if he wanted to kill or kiss his uncle.

"I've got plans, unfortunately," Dylan said. He wasn't ready to pitch the ranch to his father yet, even though it was probably a good time to do that.

"With LeAnn?" his uncle asked. "Bring her along."

Oh hell no. Not yet. That was also too soon. He needed more time to prepare himself. At least a week. Besides, there was Lola to think about. "I can't. We've made plans to take Lola to Last Stand. I need to give her a few months to rest."

"You need a horse, son?" his father asked.

Dylan's pride fought with his practicality. He couldn't ride Lola in any more events this year. But he needed to win as many as he could to keep saving for the ranch and for Lola's keep.

"Yeah," Dylan said.

"I think I can rent you one," Lou said. "For a percentage of your winnings."

Dylan's lips twitched in a reluctant smile. "You got it."

His father held out his hand. "Come and visit the next time you're in the area. Your mother misses you."

He shook his father's hand, and then hugged his mother—being careful to avoid hurting his ribs. "Yeah," Dylan said, surprising himself. "I will."

Chapter Sixteen

DYLAN WAS ONE hurtin' puppy by the time the rodeo ended. He was having a hard time keeping his eyes open.

"If you want, you can sleep in the Winnebago," LeAnn said.

"No, I'm not going to let you do this long drive all by yourself." Dylan's ribs were on fire. They were heavily taped up, but he had been lucky. They weren't cracked, they were just sore as hell.

"Well, then I'm driving." LeAnn crossed her arms over her chest, and he was distracted at how it pushed her luscious breasts up. His ribs didn't hurt that bad, he told himself. But when he moved toward her too quickly, he was rewarded with a stabbing pain.

Shit. Maybe he should take it easy.

"Fine. Have it your way," he said.

"I think you mean, thank you," she said pertly.

Yeah, he did. "Thank you, sweetheart." He kissed her quickly on the mouth.

Luckily Dolly and Reba were there to help them get Lola situated in the trailer. While LeAnn said her goodbyes to her sisters, Dylan pulled himself into the passenger seat of the truck, making himself as comfortable as he could. When his phone rang and he saw that it was Mr. Hitchcock, he answered it. "Hello."

"LeAnn put on a good show today," Mr. Hitchcock said.

LeAnn had stayed on for eight seconds. It wasn't the best time of all the ladies, but it was the first time she had completed a ride during the exhibitions. There hadn't been time for him to congratulate her yet, but they had the long drive to Last Stand ahead of them to connect again after the craziness of the past few days.

"It's a good sign of how she's going to do when it really counts, isn't it?" Mr. Hitchcock said.

"I hope so," Dylan said. Starting at the next event in Tulsa, the scores would count to qualify for the finals in Las Vegas in October. She had four months of hard competition ahead of her. Callie and Muriel were the better riders. LeAnn was a solid third place, though. He wasn't sure how to break that to LeAnn yet. He was afraid that if he mentioned his doubts, LeAnn would go over the top with her training and he'd have another Johnny Montana on his hands. Then again, was he really one to talk about taking risks? Fever Dream had been a big risk on his part.

"You had a hell of a ride, too. Got banged up a bit, didn't you?"

"I'll be all right," Dylan said.

"Do you have any good tips for me for Oklahoma's events?" Mr. Hickory said eagerly.

"Not yet," Dylan said. "I'll know more when we get there."

"That's cutting it close."

"I'll see what I can do." Dylan pushed aside his uneasiness about this line of questioning. Mr. Hickory was his boss and was paying him a generous salary to watch over his bulls, not give him gambling tips. "The bulls look good," he said, hopefully changing the subject.

"That's good to hear," Mr. Hickory said. "I need you to be my eyes and ears, though. Not only with the bulls but for everything that's going on. I stand to make a lot of money placing insider bets. I don't like to lose."

"They call it gambling for a reason, Mr. Hickory. Nothing's guaranteed." Dylan smiled at LeAnn as she got the car. "And I hate to see you lose your money."

LeAnn looked over at him quizzically, but he shook his head.

"I'd hate to lose it more," Mr. Hickory said. "I like that you're careful, man, but I didn't get where I am today by not taking risks. I'm paying you to mitigate those risks. I'll touch base with you in Oklahoma."

Dylan wanted to remind him that he was paying him to evaluate the bulls, not be a spy. But that wasn't a conversation he wanted to have with LeAnn in the truck. "See you then."

"Who was that?" LeAnn asked.

"Mr. Hickory."

"How's the job going?"

"It's a steady paycheck," Dylan said.

"Fingers crossed that we'll get another one," she said. "Dolly seems convinced she can convince Sierra Boots to sponsor us."

"That would take a lot of financial worry off me," he said. "I could maybe even bank my salary from Hickory Livestock to save up for the ranch."

"It really helped that they were watching when we both rode well today. I was even wearing my Sierra Boots. Too bad they pinch like hell."

"You had a great ride today," he said. "I'm sorry I wasn't there to see it. My parents and uncle came to visit and since I wasn't going to go out to dinner with them, I was kind of stuck showing them around."

"No worries. I understand."

"Maybe next time, we could go out to dinner with them?" he said.

"I'd like that. I won't subject you to my parents yet. I'll let you get used to my sisters' brand of crazy first."

"They seem okay to me. Dolly is…well…Dolly. Reba, on the other had…" He trailed off. "I think she just needed to get used to me."

"Yeah," LeAnn said. "Reba's had a rough go of it with men. At her old job, she had a nightmare of a boss and it's made her a little skittish. Around animals, she's the best. She doesn't warm up to people right away, though. But I think she likes you. Both my sisters like you."

"I like them too. I was wondering if they'd blame me for you not winning more."

LeAnn snorted. "They know better than that. And even if they didn't, anyone with eyes can see that I'm improving. I finally feel that it's all coming together. I finally broke that losing streak."

"Just keep in mind, you need to start small and work

your way up. You can't rush the experience, or you risk backsliding on any progress you make."

"I know," she said. "But I also know that even a good ride isn't a win if you get a lousy bull." She cocked a glance at him. "I'm hoping that our bulls get stronger and more challenging to ride."

"They'll improve when you do," Dylan said.

"Harsh," LeAnn said, sticking her tongue out at him.

"But true."

"All right. I'll give you that. Just let me enjoy this victory, okay?"

"You've earned it. I'll buy you a beer when we get to Last Stand. There's a bed-and-breakfast there, if I remember correctly. Do you want to spend our evening there and get started on the road to Tulsa fresh tomorrow morning?"

"About that," she said. "Dolly and Reba are going to take the Winnebago and Garth's trailer straight to Oklahoma. It's just going to be you and me for the next couple days."

"That sounds nice," Dylan said. And it did. "We can split up the drive tomorrow and take our time getting there. We'll make frequent stops and just enjoy the scenery and each other."

"I'd love that," she said, sneaking him a kiss at the stoplight. "It's been lonely driving from rodeo to rodeo all by myself."

"Why isn't one of your sisters with you?" He reached down and took two Cokes out of the small beverage cooler. His ribs didn't thank him for that. Patting down his pockets, he fished out a bottle of ibuprofen and took two.

"Sometimes they are. Sometimes they're together in the truck. Dolly's usually on her phone anyway."

"I missed you this week," he said, reaching out to hold her hand.

"You saw me every day." A cute blush flushed over her pink cheeks.

"Yeah, but I didn't get to wrap your legs around my face and taste you until you came on my tongue."

"Dylan," she half-shrieked as she blushed crimson to the roots of her hair. "I'm going to run off the road if you keep saying things like that." Dylan could see her nipples had hardened to little peaks through her thin cotton shirt.

"I want to make love to you all night long. I want to wake up in the morning with you in my arms and after another round of lovemaking, take a shower with you before we head out to a pancake breakfast."

She gave a deep appreciative sigh. "That sounds like heaven. I can't wait to spend the night with you like a normal couple. Just you and me."

"You know what else I want?" he asked.

"I'll pull this truck over if you don't behave," she warned.

It was tempting, but he knew his ribs couldn't take having her in the cramped truck cabin. But he thought long and hard about it. Maybe if it wasn't broad daylight, he reasoned. He decided to bring the conversation back from being seconds away from an indecent exposure charge from a state trooper.

"I want barbecue for dinner with a giant slice of peach pie for dessert." Dylan could almost taste it.

"I know just the place for that in Last Stand," she said.

"And let's skip the bed-and breakfast. We can get a nice hotel room."

"That sounds nice," LeAnn said. "But I think I can do even better. There's a retreat center on the Three Sisters Ranch that's run by one of the Sullivan sisters. Janice said she had a room available for us. It's got a hot tub, and it comes with breakfast the next morning."

"Is it expensive?" he asked. "I don't mean to be a cheapskate, but until I see how Lola is healing, I'll need to be a little frugal with my winnings."

"It's their off-season. I booked it at a really good rate."

Dylan straightened uncomfortably in his seat.

"You can get the hotel bill, the next time," she said in a long-suffering tone.

He needed to work on being grateful for having someone like her in his life. "I like the idea of a next time. And yeah, it will be nice to soak in a hot tub." He leaned over and kissed her. "Thank you."

"There, that wasn't so hard, was it?"

"It'll be a lot harder tonight," he promised, loving the slight blush on her cheek.

They drove awhile in silence. He was about to doze off when she spoke.

"So, I should tell you…Mick has been a dick lately," LeAnn blurted out.

"What did that asshole do now? Do you want me to kick the shit out of him?"

"No, I want to kick the shit out of him," she said. "But what good would that do?"

"It might make you feel better. It would make me feel better."

"He's not worth it," she said, giving him a sidelong glance.

"Why do I get the feeling that Mick is going to get my foot up his ass sooner rather than later?" Dylan asked.

"He warned me about having you as a coach the other day. He said you caused Johnny Montana's death."

Dylan closed his eyes and leaned his head back on the headrest. He wondered why she hadn't brought up Johnny before now. "A lot of people believe that."

"I didn't know you were coaching him. That must have been horrible for you when he died." She squeezed his hand in sympathy.

"It was horrible for a lot of people," Dylan said.

"I asked Dolly about it. I would have asked you, but this week has been crazy, and I didn't want to distract you from your ride with Fever Dream."

Shrugging, Dylan opened his eyes so he wouldn't have to see the movie of Johnny's last wreck that his mind played over and over again on the insides of his eyelids. "It's always there, so it's not much of a distraction."

"Was it hard to take on another student?"

"It was harder that it was you," he said.

"I'm sorry," she said softly.

"Don't be. You're a different rider than Johnny was. You have different bulls available to you than he did."

"I knew it," she said, thumping her hand on the steering wheel. "You're giving us weak-ass bulls."

"I'm recommending bulls that are suited to your riding

skills. Do you think you could have ridden Fever Dream?" Dylan watched her as she stewed over that.

"I would have liked the chance to try. I've got to ride a bigger bull sometime."

"Absolutely," he agreed. "But like I've been saying, you need to work up to it. Get more practice in on the smaller bulls."

"It's hard to wait," she said. "I feel like I'm ready."

"Johnny felt like he was ready too," Dylan said. "And it might have been what killed him." He had picked a bull that would show what he was made of, much in the same way Dylan had picked Fever Dream.

"Everybody wrecks. That's why I always wear the chest protector and helmet. The sport was a lot more deadly when we didn't wear those things."

"The gear doesn't mean squat if you land wrong or the bull lands on you. Johnny hit his head just right and snapped his neck."

"Then it wasn't your fault," she said.

Dylan shrugged. "You second-guess yourself. Was there something I could've told him to make the landing any easier? Could he have stayed on the bull, and not have fallen off if I had been a better trainer? Should I have recommended that he pick another bull?" Dylan blew out a breath. "Logic and emotion don't have a place when it comes to something like this." He thought back on his own parents' decision to keep him safe by sending him to his uncle's farm. "His parents haven't forgiven me."

LeAnn squeezed his hand. "It's so unfair that they're taking their grief out on you. If they need someone to blame, why don't they blame the damned bull?"

"They did. They bought the bull for ten thousand dollars and then shot it."

LeAnn shuddered. "I hope it brought them peace."

"It wasn't the bull's fault either. I mean it was, but that's what bulls are trained to do—buck and fuss. Johnny wouldn't have wanted them to kill the bull, but I guess it was better the bull got shot instead of me." He tried for a smile, but failed.

"Out of all the rides that go on throughout all of the rodeos in this country, someone dying on a bull is about as common as that same person dying in a car crash. At least that's how I look at it," LeAnn said. "I'm more in danger when I get behind the wheel of the Winnebago after a hard day of riding."

Dylan leaned his head back and gave her a more realistic smile. "Yeah, but the Winnebago isn't trying to eject you from the driver seat by blowing doughnuts on the highway."

"No, but the other drivers can be just as crazy as a bull."

"True. But that's not going to stop me from worrying about you. I care about you, and it kills me that I might have to watch you get hurt. But I know that you're going to do this with or without me. I'm a good coach and I can make you a better rider. So, I push my feelings aside when you're out on the bull…even though it makes me want to puke with anxiety."

LeAnn sagged in her seat. "I wish I could make it easier."

"Every ride it gets a little easier. If you win, it'll be all worth it."

"What if I don't win?" she asked forlornly.

"Don't even think like that."

"I've sacrificed my barrel racing. My bronc racing. I've got to win this, or I'll be right back where I started three years ago when I lost to Merry and took up with Mick."

Dylan thought about sharing his feelings that she was a solid third in ranking, and that was still a hell of an achievement in a new event, but he didn't think that would help the way she was feeling right now. LeAnn wanted to be number one, and he wasn't sure he'd be able to get her there. Johnny had also thought that he wasn't progressing as fast as he should have been, so he took more risks. Chose deadlier bulls. Chased victory at the cost of his own body. LeAnn had that same drive inside her. At the end of the season, if she was still in third, Dylan wondered if he'd be another regret in her life.

Chapter Seventeen

Last Stand, TX

LEANN PULLED INTO the Three Sisters Ranch just after suppertime. Janice Sullivan told them to help themselves to any leftovers in the retreat center's fridge, but Dylan had put the idea of barbecue and peach pie in her head and nothing else was going to work for dinner. After securing Lola in the barn and going over her treatment with Janice, they tossed their overnight bags into their room and headed out to the Draeger Peach Haus for dinner and pie. Stuffed and exhausted, they were back at the retreat center in a few hours.

"Last one in the hot tub is a rotten egg," LeAnn said.

"And me without my bathing suit." Dylan grinned.

"Whatever shall we do then?" LeAnn shucked off her clothes, tossing them on the floor as the hot tub filled up. She poured in some scented crystals while Dylan also got undressed and put a toiletry bag next to the bed. When the water was hot enough, she sat in and let it fill up around her while she admired Dylan's body, even if he had a few ugly-looking bruises on his ribs that were a mottled purple black and yellow.

"I think I see the outline of Fever Dream's hooves on

your chest. That looks painful," she said.

"It is. I hope that you never have to experience it."

"You and me both."

Dylan set up his phone to play some George Strait love songs. Grabbing the bottle of wine that Janice had left in their room, he opened it and poured two glasses.

He winced as he eased into the hot tub next to her. She loved feeling his body so close to hers and couldn't help stroking his arm tenderly. He looked down at her with admiration mixed with lust. It made her toes curl in anticipation.

"I wish it could be like this for us every night."

"This is perfect," she said. "But it always is. I don't need a fancy room. I just need you."

"To us." Dylan clicked his glass to hers. He gave her a quick kiss and his lips were far sweeter than the wine. Her heart thudded in her chest. She was falling in love with this man and she was helpless to do anything about it. Truthfully, she didn't want to stop the feelings. It was odd though, to want something more than what the rodeo could give her.

She wondered if he felt the same way. LeAnn was going to think of this night as the start of their relationship. Sure, they had slept together before. And it had been wild and wonderful. But tonight, with George Strait crooning about checking yes or no, this was different. Tonight, anything was possible.

"I'm glad I don't have to go home tonight," she said.

"Me too."

The water shut off automatically and the jets pulsed on,

filling the tub around them with fragrant bubbles that held notes of sandalwood and patchouli. When they finished the wine, LeAnn was feeling sleepy from soaking in the tub. Leaning her head against Dylan's chest, she enjoyed the moment of peace.

"Are you falling asleep on me, sweetheart?" Dylan asked.

"No." LeAnn yawned.

"Come on, let's get you dried off and into bed. Normally, I'd carry you out, but I don't think my ribs could take it. Not tonight anyway."

"Just pretend I'm a calf." She took the hand he held out to help her out of the tub.

"Too bad I left my rope in the truck," he said.

"That's a shame," she said, giving him an exaggerated wink.

"Is that right?" he growled, holding her close to his naked body as he walked her back to the bed. They got under the covers, kissing the whole time. This was her favorite part of being with Dylan. He was a great kisser. The soft way his mouth stroked hers tingled, then grew to a fever pitch that soon had her pressing desperately against him, wanting, needing him to kiss her harder, touch her more, and make her his.

She parted her thighs for Dylan's fingers and whimpered eagerly as they tickled against all of her sensitive places. His mouth devoured hers as he brought her closer and closer to the elusive ecstasy that was just out of her reach. When he kissed down to her chest and latched on to her nipple, LeAnn spiraled out of control. She clamped her thighs around his hand and let the waves of pleasure flow through her as he sucked hard on her nipple, strumming the tip with his tongue.

He started off slow. Every touch of Dylan's hand felt as soft as a butterfly's wing caressing her oversensitive nerve endings. LeAnn knew she couldn't take much more of the sweet torture. She wanted to feel the calloused roughness of his palms over her curves, feel him clutch her backside possessively as he licked eagerly between her thighs.

"Please," she murmured, lifting her hips up to his waiting mouth. When his tongue touched her core, it felt like skyrockets danced behind her eyelids. LeAnn stretched lethargically, loving the rasp of his beard against her inner thighs. Incoherent now with pleasure, she could only murmur the word "Oh," over and over again. As his talented tongue danced over her sensitive folds, touching the responsive bundle of nerves at the juncture of her thighs, LeAnn knew she'd never forget this night. She wanted this glorious feeling to last forever. She wanted to remember the softness of the sheets, and the spicy musk of the sandalwood and patchouli that still clung to their bodies after the bath. The erotic sound of him lapping at her wetness helped her tumble endlessly into oblivion.

She wasn't sure how long she lay there, stunned and floating from sensual overload. LeAnn was dimly aware of him kissing back up her body.

"Dylan," she whispered, trying to push him back so that she could return the favor. After a few more long kisses, he relented, lying back.

"Be gentle with me," he joked.

Avoiding the bruised area of his ribs, aside from a tender brush of her fingers, LeAnn kissed his hip and then eagerly gripped him in her hands. She stroked him once, twice, loving the way he felt.

Dylan hissed in pleasure and his eyes rolled back. "You do that so well," he said. "I could come just by watching you."

"Okay," she said softly and continued to stroke him, every now and then leaning over to lick the tip.

Unable to resist not being able to taste him, she took him deep in her throat, moving swiftly up and down his shaft. His fingers were rough in her hair, tugging and pulling, but that just drove her wilder. He finished down her throat with a strangled grunt and a whispered fervent prayer, "LeAnn, sweetheart."

Now it was his turn to lie spent and panting on the sheets. Reaching into his toiletry bag, he pulled out a condom and wordlessly handed it to her. "If you don't mind doing all the work, I'll make it up to you once my ribs are back in fighting condition."

"My pleasure," she said. And it would be. Rolling the condom down his thick hard length, she positioned herself over him. Easing his shaft inside her, LeAnn sank down on his hardness. As always, he filled her deep and tight. She had to take a quick breath as her body adjusted around him.

"I'll be gentle," she said breathlessly, and began to move so that the friction built up slow and easy between them as she softly bounced on him. He cupped her swaying breasts in his palms and thumbed her nipples, pinching and tugging lightly when she picked up the pace, needing to feed the beast that was growing within her.

The bedsprings creaked as the headboard rocked back against the wall. She was chanting his name now, mindless in the pleasure his body was giving her.

"That's it, sweetheart," he said. "Come for me. Let me see you lose control." Dylan's voice was shaky and breathless. LeAnn knew he was moments behind her. Gripping his shoulders, she forgot to be careful. He didn't seem to mind as his fingers tightened around her hips. She wanted him to leave marks. She wanted him to mark her as his.

"Dylan," she screamed as a forceful orgasm shook through her, weakening her limbs and sapping her strength. She remembered in time to roll off him, so she didn't put any more pressure on his bruised ribs.

"Was I too rough?" she whispered, pressing a kiss on his bicep.

"You were perfect," Dylan said. "Just perfect."

Chapter Eighteen

Tulsa, Oklahoma

THE RIDE TO Oklahoma wasn't the usual chore with LeAnn sitting next to him. They had an early start with breakfast at the retreat center. Fueled up on bacon, eggs, and pancakes, Dylan went over to the barn to check on Lola one last time.

"This isn't goodbye," Dylan promised her. "I won't be able to get that ranch we were looking at, but there'll be another one. And then, you'll have all the hay you want and wide-open spaces to roam around all day." He patted her neck and rested his forehead on hers. Dylan was going to miss her, but he was more than pleased with the surroundings and the level of care that she was going to get at the Three Sisters Ranch.

"We'll take good care of her," Janice Sullivan had said, shaking his hand.

"I appreciate that."

Like they had planned, they took several rest breaks. Stopping for a picnic lunch at a rest stop wasn't very romantic, but it felt good to stretch his legs and to feel the sun on his face. LeAnn even flipped through the binder he had put together about ideas for the horse ranch.

"You should put this on the computer, so you don't lose it."

"I will," he said. "But I like the feel of the paper. It seems more real when it's actually in front of me instead of electronically on a screen. Besides," he said, "some of the motels I stay in have crappy internet service."

"Have you ever thought about finding an investor or a partner?" she asked.

He made a face. "I'd rather do it on my own, but I might consider it if things got desperate."

"What did your parents say when you told them about it?"

"I haven't yet," he said with a shrug. "I need to practice what to say to them. I've got to counter all the arguments my father is going to throw at me because I'm only going to have one chance."

"Maybe we should buy lottery tickets instead."

"Maybe." And the next time they filled up, he bought two. One for her and one for him. "We'll split it if we win."

"Deal," she said.

By the time they got to Tulsa, the ache in his chest from missing Lola gave way to the standard aches and the pain in his ribs. He wouldn't have been roping at this event anyway, but he still missed his horse. His uncle wouldn't be at another rodeo until Montana, so he was only bull riding for the Oklahoma events. It wouldn't kill him to take it easy. But it would be a burden on his wallet until he signed the contract with Sierra Boots—if Dolly could work her magic. With a fifteen percent commission, she was probably very motivated to do that.

"Are you sure that you'll be able to ride a bull? Are your ribs okay?" LeAnn asked.

"I'll tape them up extra good. It won't be fun, but I'll be all right." He was a little annoyed that his knee was starting to twinge and lock up as well. It felt like a ticking clock, letting him know how much time he had left in the rodeo game.

Dylan needed to win, though. He needed the points to keep himself in the running for the all-around standings to qualify for the large grand prize from the MPRC at the end of the season. He had six more states and three times that many rodeos at the very least in order to qualify.

"How are you feeling today about your ride?" Dylan asked.

"Good, although I think Muriel and Callie have the better bulls."

"Maybe," Dylan said, looking over the roster. "But all these bulls are still so new, any one of them could surprise us."

"You're not giving me easy bulls because you're afraid I'll end up like Johnny, are you?"

Dylan was a little annoyed that she had asked that, but he figured it was a fair question. He thought about it for a moment and answered as honestly as he could. "I'm recommending bulls that will match your skill level, same as I do the other women riders. These are just suggestions, but keep in mind this is my job. Mr. Hickory wants me to evaluate the WPRC bulls to make sure that no rider gets on a bull that they can't handle."

"I want to try tougher bulls," she said.

"You just started staying on for eight seconds. You need more practice."

"Don't hold me back because you're afraid I'll get hurt."

"While I would like to wrap you in cotton wool and have you mutton bust instead of bronc busting, you'd hate me for it. I know that because if anybody ever did that to me, I would resent it. You can trust me. I only have your safety and best interests in mind when I suggest which bulls go into the drawings that you choose from." And if he erred on the side of caution, especially with her, Dylan felt it was worth it to make sure she was safe.

LeAnn's face softened. "I didn't mean to imply that I couldn't trust you. I'm sorry. I guess I'm just a little nervous. When I see the scores and the rankings, I know I'm not the best."

There it was again. He had an obligation as her coach to set her expectations. But he found he couldn't crush the spark of hope he saw in her eyes. "Yet," Dylan said. "You've got eighteen more rodeos to qualify for the finals." He was confident that she would make it into the finals. Once she got there, however, she didn't have a prayer of beating Callie or Muriel if her riding stayed the same. But Vegas was still a ways away, and anything could happen.

IT HADN'T BEEN a bad day at the rodeo. Both he and LeAnn stayed on their bulls for eight seconds. LeAnn actually placed second in bronc busting, and third in barrel racing. Then her sister Dolly had whisked her away to talk to a bunch of sponsors. Sierra Boots hadn't scheduled a meeting with them yet, so Dolly wasn't putting all of her eggs into one basket.

Dylan texted LeAnn, asking her to let him know when she was done, and then they could discuss what they wanted to do tonight. Reba and Dolly were still living in the RV with LeAnn, so that left her place out. He hadn't booked a room yet, because he wanted to be frugal with his money until he was back competing at all the events.

While he waited for her to get free, he walked down the road to a greasy spoon that the local boys said had the best fried okra. Not wanting to hold up a table, Dylan went into the large bar where a few of the bullfighters were playing pool. He texted LeAnn the address and a copy of the menu with the note:

Should I order?

When she didn't get back to him, Dylan ordered a beer and sat at the bar. As he nursed it, he scrolled through websites on his phone to search for land auctions, trying to see what the going rates were and how much was required for down payment. His best bet might be to acquire land at an auction, but to do that, he needed to have serious money in the bank first. He knew the smart thing to do was to wait a year or two and try again for the loan, but he didn't want to wait. The longer he waited, the harder it would be to save. Lola's boarding fees would eat into his profits. When he bought a new horse, that would eat into his profits too.

He was brooding about that when Mick came into the bar. Dylan didn't acknowledge him and went back to his phone. As long as Mick didn't say shit about LeAnn and kept minding his own business, Dylan could pretend that Mick didn't exist.

Again, Dylan had to wonder—if he had made different choices in his life, would things be different now? Of course, it was ridiculous to try and "what if" his life. If he wasn't in the rodeo, he wouldn't have to worry about Lola. And maybe if he had been smarter and got better grades in school, he would have followed in his father's footsteps and become a venture capitalist.

Dylan snorted at the thought. Not likely.

All he needed was one good break. So that meant he had to stay healthy for the rest of the season, but still take enough risks so that he could outride Mick and the rest of the bull riders. If he could do that, and get Sierra Boots as a sponsor, he might be able to afford a down payment on the ranch sooner rather than later. And once he could show the bank that he had steady employment, he might be able to swing that loan to buy a ranch at auction next year.

Of course, if he swallowed his pride and asked his parents for money, his father might give him a loan now. Dylan could probably convince him it was a good investment. Before he could think about it, he dialed his father's number.

"Hey, Dad," he said when the voicemail picked up. "I wanted to discuss a project I had in mind with you. Uncle Lou mentioned it. It's about a rescue ranch I want to start up. I'll email you the business plans and we can discuss it when you get a minute. Thanks. Love to you and Mom."

When he hung up, he felt like he had just gone eight seconds. Of course, he wasn't sure if he'd wrecked or scored big. He guessed he'd find out.

Debbi Peterson came in and went over to Mick. She was a barrel racer, but from what he could recall about the women's scores, she wasn't any competition for LeAnn. It looked like Mick and Debbi were together and that was a bit of a relief. It would keep Mick from trying to reconnect with LeAnn.

Speaking of which, where the heck was she? He checked his phone, but she hadn't gotten back to him. All he wanted was to sit down with LeAnn and grab dinner and a couple of smooches. It would be the perfect way to end the busy day. They had practice tomorrow morning before heading out to the next town. So it would have to be an early night, but he was ready for it.

A few more people from the rodeo filtered in and grabbed tables. He eyeballed some baskets of fried chicken and okra and was hard pressed not to place an order.

About a half hour later, though, LeAnn came in. He was happy to note that her whole face lit up when she saw him. The fact that Mick was scowling at that from across the room made it even better. When she came in to give him a hug, Dylan couldn't help giving her a deep kiss to show her how much he missed her.

"What was that for?" LeAnn asked as a blush crept up her cheeks.

"I wanted to. And because I was staking a claim."

Her eyebrows shot up to her hairline. "A claim?"

"Don't look now, but Mick is headed over here."

"No fighting," she warned.

Dylan put a hand over his heart. "I will not throw the first punch."

"So you're trying to steal Sierra Boots and LeAnn out from under me," Mick said.

When Dylan laughed in his face, LeAnn bristled. "I am not yours to steal."

But Mick didn't even acknowledge her. "You knew that Sierra Boots was looking for a couple. It was supposed to be me with her, not you."

LeAnn folded her arms over her chest and glared at Mick. "I don't want to be with you. Not even for a pretend magazine spread. I want to be with my real boyfriend. Because he cares about me and believes in me."

Dylan felt a twinge of guilt about keeping his feelings of her chances at winning in Vegas to himself.

"He believes in you because you're paying him," Mick said.

Dylan set down his beer. That was about enough. He started rolling up his sleeves.

"LeAnn, he's going to get you hurt. He got Johnny Montana killed. I don't want to see that happen to you."

That son of a bitch. Dylan stood up. LeAnn put a warning hand on his chest.

"Oh bullshit," she said. "Johnny's death was a tragedy. But Dylan had nothing to do with it."

"He was his coach."

"It was a bad bull, on a bad day, on a bad ride," LeAnn said. "It could have happened to anyone."

"And a bad fall," a new voice said.

Oh crap. How had Dylan not seen *him*?

"Stay out of this," Mick said, pointing a warning finger at him.

"Can't do that," Bobby Montana said. "Johnny was my brother."

Mick blinked in surprise "Well, I guess you want to get in a couple of punches for your brother's sake. Feel free. My only condition is the girl doesn't get hurt."

"I'll take that advantage," LeAnn said. "Because you're not going to hurt Dylan. Not on my watch."

"Stop hiding behind her skirt," Mick said.

It was a little embarrassing that she thought he needed help. But truthfully, he was outnumbered. Dylan didn't want LeAnn in a fight, but he also didn't want her to get pissed at him for telling her again to stay out of it.

"You tell her to back off. She doesn't listen to me," Dylan said.

"I'm not listening to any of y'all," LeAnn said. "This can't happen. Mick, you're trying to sabotage our chance with Sierra Boots." She looked around as if she expected the sponsor to pop out of one of the back booths. "Let's just get out of here before things get ugly."

"It's already ugly," Mick said.

Bobby walked up to Dylan, and Dylan tensed for the blow. Fighting against Mick was one thing. Fighting against a brother mourning his dead kin was another. He straightened and stuck his chin out.

"Take your shot," Dylan said, and dropped his hands. He wasn't surprised that Mick rushed in to take advantage of his hands being down, but he was surprised when Bobby turned and met Mick's charge with a fist in his face. Bobby followed it up with another one to the nose, and a shot to the stomach for good measure.

It was over before it began. Dylan didn't know whether to be relieved or disappointed.

"Get the hell out of here," the bartender said, then pointed at Mick. "And take him with you."

"Sorry for the mess." Dylan put a few twenties on the bar.

He and Bobby pulled a dry-heaving Mick up by his armpits and dragged him out into the parking lot. Dylan's ribs weren't thanking him for the extra activity, so maybe it was a good thing he and Mick hadn't gotten into it. Then they walked away from Mick, who was still trying to get back to his feet.

"I appreciate the help. I'd have thought you would have taken a shot at me," Dylan said, still puzzled that Bobby hadn't. Reaching down, he entwined his fingers with LeAnn's.

"That's not me. Besides, my father gave you a hard enough time. I wanted to apologize for his behavior."

"He's entitled to his anger," Dylan said.

"Yeah, but not at you. Johnny had nothing but good words to say about you, and he improved under your coaching."

Something tight in Dylan's chest started to unravel at Bobby words. He hadn't known that he needed to hear those words until Bobby said them.

"Dad doesn't really blame you. None of us do. As time

goes by, I think he'll see that. I just want to let you know you don't have to worry about him. My mother made him promise not to go to any more rodeos."

"I'm sorry he won't be there to watch you win events."

Bobby shrugged. "It means I don't have to listen to him when I lose. I'm never going to do rodeo as a career. I'm not that talented. I have a job. I work Monday through Friday and travel to the local shows. I can't travel all the time, like you guys do. But I like it, and it's fun, even though it did take my brother from me."

"You've got talent," Dylan said. "Don't give up on your dream to be a rodeo star."

Bobby gave a half-smile. "That was more my brother's dream. My dream is to ask my girl to marry me and settle down in a nice house and raise a couple kids."

"That's a good dream," LeAnn said.

Dylan bit back a sigh. It was a good dream, but one he couldn't provide for LeAnn. It felt like he didn't deserve her loyalty.

"I can't do that traveling from rodeo to rodeo."

His words hit Dylan in the gut worse than Mick's fist would have. He nodded. "I get that." And he did, because he'd chosen the traveling rodeo life over settling down for the last ten years or so. He'd been doing rodeo for so long, Dylan didn't know anything else. Maybe this job with Mr. Hickory's bulls would allow him to settle down, but then, maybe it wouldn't. For now, at least, Dylan still had a few good rides left in him to try and make his fortune.

"My brother didn't know when to quit," Bobby continued. "Most of time, that was a good thing. But he had no business being on that bull and he knew it. He told me that you didn't want him to ride it, and he thought that you were holding him back out of jealousy."

"I had no idea he felt that way." Dylan shook his head. "That wasn't the case at all."

"I saw that because I had some distance from it. But Johnny would never have been able to understand. I'm not saying that what happened to Johnny was inevitable, but had he listened to you and your coaching, maybe he would have been alive today. And that's on him—not on you. I just wanted to let you know that."

"Thank you," Dylan said, his throat tightening with emotion. "That means a lot."

They heard police sirens, and the serious mood was broken.

"Do you think someone called the cops on us?" LeAnn asked, her hand still firmly in his.

"Let's not take that chance," Bobby said.

"Agreed." After shaking Bobby's hand one last time, Dylan asked LeAnn, "Is your truck here?"

"No. Reba dropped me off."

"Then we're hoofing it back to the rodeo grounds. Are you up for some dinner? I was hoping for Oklahoma's best okra, but we got kicked out of the joint."

LEANN WAS IN mid-chew of the best damned burger she had eaten in a while when Dolly started blowing up her phone.

"I'd better get this," she said after swallowing and wiping away the greasy goodness on her fingers with her napkin. "Don't eat all the onion rings."

Dylan's mouth was too full to reply.

"What's up?" she said.

"How could you do this to me?" Dolly wailed. Her sister sounded in tears.

"What? What's wrong?"

"Sierra Boots told us to fuck off because of that stunt you and Dylan pulled."

"What stunt? Dolly, you're not making sense."

"Check out the rodeo's forums and Mick's social media."

"Oh no, what did he do?"

Dylan frowned and peered over as she brought up Mick's accounts.

"This is a lie," LeAnn said.

Mick was posting pictures of his swollen face and bloody nose. *"Dylan Porter sucker-punched me over LeAnn Keller."*

"Dolly, it's bullshit. Dylan never laid a hand on him."

"Is that right? Check the pictures on the forums."

Switching over to the WPRC forum, she saw a picture of herself standing between Mick and Dylan. It looked like she was holding Dylan back. And of course, that miserable bitch Debbi Peterson was talking shit about her all over the boards, saying that LeAnn had been egging the men on to fight over her. She also was collaborating Mick's story.

"I swear, this isn't what it looks like. We're being framed."

"You're in a bar, LeAnn. In the middle of a bar fight."

"It was a restaurant. I didn't have a drink. Mick was the aggressor."

"Who roughed him up?"

"Bobby Montana, Johnny's brother. Mick was talking shit. It wasn't Dylan."

Dolly sighed. "I believe you. Unfortunately, no one else does. So you can kiss this sponsor goodbye."

"Dolly, I'm so sorry," she said. It was happening again. Only this time, she hadn't mooned anyone. She hadn't done anything wrong, but no one would believe it. Not with her past. And Sierra Boots—and their fifty thousand dollars—was off the table.

"Me too."

When Dolly hung up, all LeAnn could do was stare at her phone. Acid churned in her stomach, making her decision to have the hamburger platter seem like a really bad idea. "How much did you hear?"

"All of it," Dylan said grimly. "If he wants to say I beat the shit out of him, I'm about to make that a reality."

"The damage has been done," she said quietly. "He knew what he was doing. He wanted to mess up this chance for us because he's a spiteful little shit."

"He'll get his," Dylan said.

"Look, I'm not feeling so well. Do you mind if we get out of here? I want to go home and see if I can make it up to Dolly."

"Sure. I'll go pay the check." Dylan got up and flagged down their waitress to meet him at the register.

This sucked. They were back to square one with their

finances. Dylan was that much further away from the ranch he wanted, and she was staring down bankruptcy if she couldn't bring in more prize money. LeAnn took a shaky breath. She'd really thought it was going to work out for her. She'd thought if she had just concentrated on the rodeo, the sponsorship would take care of itself. But Sierra Boots wanted an image that was just not her. It could have been, though. If she had changed herself, and played the role they wanted her to play for the entire year. Maybe that asshole Mick and his little bitch Debbi had done her and Dylan a favor.

After Dylan drove her back to the Winnebago, he gave her a long hug and kissed her sweetly.

"Do you want to come in?" she asked, her toes curling in those damned uncomfortable boots.

"No, I don't want to rile Dolly up any more than she is already."

"Where are you staying tonight?"

"I'm just going to sleep in the truck. I'll meet you in Guthrie tomorrow morning for practice."

"Yeah," she said. She would just have to practice harder. If Sierra Boots didn't want her, that didn't mean another sponsor wouldn't snap her up if she won more events.

He stroked her cheek and she leaned into the caress. She wished they were staying in a hotel together, but it was probably for the best that they saved the money for gas. "Sweet dreams, sweetheart. Don't let this get you down."

"I'll be all right," she said. She hoped. She watched him drive away and then with a deep shuddering sigh, she walked into the Winnebago.

She was surprised to see Dolly, Reba, and Merry Grayson crammed around their tiny dinner table doing shots.

"There she is," Merry said, and poured her a glass of Fireball whiskey.

"I'm sorry," LeAnn said and hugged Dolly.

"Hey, easy come, easy go." Dolly hiccupped.

"Here's hoping Mick gets hemorrhoids," Reba said, clinking glasses with all of them.

"Or a blistering case of herpes," Merry chimed in.

"Intense gastric distress," Dolly slurred.

"All of the above." LeAnn drank her shot.

She sank on to her bed.

"Look on the bright side," Merry said, waving the bottle. "At least you get to drink."

LeAnn tried for a smile and failed.

Sitting next to her, Reba slung her arm around her shoulder and hugged her. "You didn't really want them as a sponsor anyway. Too many rules. It would have been like living with Mom and Dad again. Remember those days?"

Rolling her eyes, LeAnn felt a smile tug at her lips. "I try not to think of it."

"And you get to kiss that hot-stuff bull rider all you want now," Merry said.

"What I'm really glad about is that I no longer have to wear these uncomfortable things." LeAnn tugged off those stupid boots and tossed them on the ground. "I was trying so hard to be what they wanted me to be. I used to be the WPRC's sweetheart."

"Then you mooned the state cop," Merry said. "It's

kind of hard to come back from flashing your ass and spending the night in the drunk tank."

"Tell me about it."

"Been there, done that." Merry grinned.

"Yeah, but you can get away with that because you're a Wild Grayson Sister."

"You just have to find out who you are. Maybe we can make you an honorary Grayson sister," Dolly said, thoughtfully.

"No," Reba said firmly. "She's *our* sister and she's just fine the way she is. To hell with Sierra Boots."

"I'll drink to that," Merry said.

"To hell with them," LeAnn agreed, clinking glasses with them again.

"There are other sponsors," Merry said. "You should try Cowboy Couture. They like a little outlaw cowgirl attitude."

"Why didn't you have them as a sponsor?" LeAnn asked.

"They wanted someone a little more family friendly."

That could be her. LeAnn looked over at Dolly, but she didn't seem to be focusing on the details right now. That was okay. They could work on that angle over the next few rodeos.

Chapter Nineteen

Montana—August

THE NEXT FEW weeks were grueling as they went from rodeo to rodeo. Some nights Dylan and LeAnn spent huddled together in a cheap hotel room. Other nights they drove in their separate trucks straight on to the next event, taking turns calling each other to make sure they both stayed awake.

Dylan was worried about LeAnn. She was winning, but she was pushing herself too hard. It was difficult not to see shades of Johnny Montana in the way she was driven to ride stronger and harder.

The arrived in Montana after spending most of the week driving so there hadn't been a lot of time to train, but he was confident that LeAnn's head was in the game. As for himself, the pain in his ribs had faded to a dull ache that never quite went away and he had developed a slight limp when it rained and his knees ached. It worried him only because the money was running out, even with his salary from Mr. Hickory, and he needed to work harder to win more events.

He stopped charging LeAnn for coaching, though. It didn't seem right now that they were in a relationship.

Besides, he had given her a binder with exercises and practice routines to go through. All she had to do was stick to it and he'd be happy to give her feedback and pointers for free.

She complained at first, but he told her he'd just spend the money on her anyway, and he would have trained her whether she was paying him or not. LeAnn made him promise to look for another coaching job, but for the moment, the salary Mr. Hickory was paying him was keeping them both afloat. The long hours on the highway were beginning to take a toll on him and all he wanted to do was sleep.

When they got to Montana, his uncle had been waiting for him with a fancy-looking horse.

"Who's this beauty?" Dylan said, rubbing the palomino's neck.

"That's Queenie. She cost a fortune, so don't break her."

"I wouldn't dream of it." She wasn't Lola and never would be, but she was young and spirited.

"She knows her stuff too. Your aunt picked her out."

"I'll call her later and thank her." Dylan didn't want to push his luck, but his father hadn't called him back. He had sent the business plan out to him a month ago. He'd called and left a message to make sure he received it, but his father hadn't responded. "Have you spoken to Dad lately?"

"Yeah, the other day. He's looking at resorts in Montego Bay to take your mom to this winter."

But he'd said nothing about the ranch. Dylan should have known not to get his hopes up. His father could have at least had the decency to turn him down rather than ghost him. But he couldn't complain, not when his uncle had just given him a gorgeous new horse to use in bulldogging and other events.

"Thanks," Dylan said.

"You can thank me with a percentage check," Lou said and gave him a wave.

Mr. Hickory had flown out to Montana and was in his spiffy brand-new cowboy boots and jeans when they met at the corral later that day. Dylan felt like an unmade bed next to him. He needed another cup of coffee and probably a shave, but it was more important to let Mr. Hickory know what he'd decided about his bulls.

"I want to move Pecos Bull up into the men's division," Dylan said. "He's developed a bit of a vicious streak."

Mr. Hickory nodded. "You're the boss. Do you want to ride him?"

"Maybe. If I pick him in the draw, I wouldn't trade. I've ridden him a few times, and he puts up a good show. But he's no Fever Dream." And thank the Lord for that.

"Fair enough," Mr. Hickory said. "I can't help but notice that LeAnn has been doing very well on her last couple of rides. I can make better money if she loses the bull-riding event this weekend. But if she wins this, I'm never going to see odds like that again."

"I wouldn't bet against her," Dylan said, scratching at the stubble on his chin. It itched.

"If you make sure she gets a bull like Pecos Bull here," Mr. Hickory said, lowering his voice and leaning into him. "I could clean up."

"I'm not going to rig the draw, so LeAnn gets a bull that she'll wreck on." He scowled at his boss.

"Yeah, I hear that you're pretty sweet on her. I get it that you don't want her hurt. How about you give her an easy one then? I could still make some money if she wins. I'd just have to bet more."

"I'm not going to spoon-feed her an easy bull either. She'd never forgive me." This conversation was making his blood boil.

"She'd never find out," Mr. Hickory said. "This would be just between you and me."

"I'd know, though, and I'd never forgive myself. I wouldn't want anybody to give me a free ride on a bull." It was one thing to be ultra-careful with the bulls that the women were riding, it was another to make sure a bull was well below their skill level to ride.

Mr. Hickory rolled his eyes. "Son, this isn't about being an athlete. This is about making money. I thought you knew the difference."

"I do know the difference and that's why I'm not going to put her on Pecos Bull or a bull that's too easy. LeAnn can win on her own merit. The women's bulls have been chosen specifically to meet their level of experience, which is what you hired me to do."

Mr. Hickory shook his head. "You disappoint me, boy."

"She's good enough to win without me fixing the results," Dylan said.

"Over Callie and Muriel?"

Dylan's jaw tightened. "It depends on the day. It depends on the bull." But the clock was ticking. They had the rest of the Montana rodeos and then all of New Mexico before the finals in Vegas. As predicted, LeAnn would be going to Vegas. But it would take a miracle for her to beat Callie and Muriel. Still, miracles could happen.

"Well, I guess that's that then." Mr. Hickory shook his hand. "I'm sorry you couldn't see it my way."

There was enough in his statement that Dylan wondered how long he'd have this job. It figured. But he didn't want to cheat, so maybe it would be best if they parted ways. After Mr. Hickory walked away, Dylan noticed that Mick had been standing close enough to overhear their conversation.

He caught Mick's eye. "Do we have a problem?"

Mick, who had been giving him a wide berth since the bar incident, shook his head and said, "No problem."

As Mick skulked away, Dylan couldn't help but feel uneasy. There was going to be a problem all right. No sense worrying about that now, though. He had to get ready for his own event.

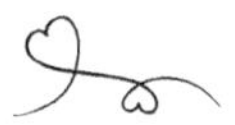

LEANN HAD JUST finished up running the barrels with Garth. Their times were excellent. She was tired, but exhilarated. Her scores were improving, and her bronc and bull rides had been the best she'd ever done. Sure, she was training more, pushing herself because when it was quiet, all her doubts and old hurts started to creep in. When she was on the back of a horse or even a bull, all of that went away. She felt free and happy.

Throughout it all, Dylan had been her rock, even when they couldn't see each other because they were traveling to different rodeos around the southwest. They usually caught up with each other on the weekends. Even though they were apart more than they were together these past weeks, LeAnn never worried that he was screwing around on her like Mick had done. It felt really good to trust in a relationship again.

Her sisters were busy with their own issues. Dolly had been called back to Texas to work her magic over in the corporate office of the WPRC. Reba was all over the place with both organizations. More often than not, she had the Winnebago and LeAnn took her truck to the events so she could spend more time with Dylan.

In the absence of her sisters, LeAnn hung out more with the bull riders—Callie, Muriel and Samantha. They'd sometimes get together at night to have a potluck dinner at Muriel's camper or sit around having drinks in the hotel bar where one of them were staying. LeAnn tried to stay away from the barrel racers, mostly because Debbi was one of them. She couldn't believe that two-faced little rat could be all sweetness and pie to her face, but as soon as LeAnn was out of earshot, she'd start up again with any shit she could stir up. And the rumor was that Sierra Boots was looking at her for their next spokesperson.

LeAnn hoped their boots gave her blisters.

LeAnn was taking care of Garth in the barn when Mick approached her. Looking around for a quick weapon, she spied one of the ropes she used for events. It wouldn't be as satisfying as a whip or anything, but still, she wouldn't want to get hit with it.

"I ought to beat you senseless and give you something to whine about on social media for real."

"Easy, Killer." Mick held up his hands in surrender.

"You've got a lot of nerve coming up to me after the bullshit you pulled. What do you want?"

"I overheard Dylan and Mr. Hickory from Hickory Livestock talking about the bull you're riding today. Apparently, you're getting two-to-one odds to win, but the payout is more if you lose."

Fuck that. "Are you going to place a bet on me?" she asked.

"I should. It's easy money with Dylan fixing the outcome."

LeAnn threw down the rope in disgust. "What are you talking about?"

"He's going to give you an easy bull to ride so you win."

"An easy bull doesn't mean a win, and you know that."

"All I know is he's in charge of making sure that you draw a better bull than everybody else."

That wasn't even remotely true, but she supposed it could be fixed up that way. The WPRC provided a list of bulls and the riders randomly picked before each event. They were allowed to trade or switch bulls with other riders. She supposed Dylan could manipulate the drawing so when it was her turn to pick, she'd get a specific bull. But it wouldn't be easy, and it would ruin the WPRC's reputation for running a fair event. But Dylan wouldn't do that. She knew that. But she also knew that she had to find a way to shut Mick up about this before the rumor mill ran with it and caused trouble for Dylan. Again.

"Mick, I'm sick of you running your mouth. I'll tell you what. When I pick my bull from the drawing pool, I'll switch it to another bull at random."

"I have a better idea. I bet you can't win on a bull of my choosing."

"Go on." She crossed her arms over her chest.

"I have a friend in the bull pens. He'll let us swap our bulls. I'll ride whatever bull you draw, and you ride whatever bull I draw."

LeAnn's pulse quickened at his words. Finally, a chance to show everyone that the women riders could use the same bulls as the men. "Why do you want to do this?"

"Lots of reasons."

"Name a few." She didn't trust him as far as she could throw him.

"I want to make Dylan look like an idiot. I want to ride an easy bull. I want you to see how dangerous it is to ride a big-boy bull." Mick ticked off the reasons on his fingers.

LeAnn rolled her eyes. "Just what is the deal with you and Dylan?"

"He got you."

"You had me, you idiot, and you threw me away."

"I never *had* you," he said, putting emphasis on the word *had*.

"You're disgusting."

"Whatever. Are we going to do this or are you too chicken?"

He wished. She'd get a chance to shut down the male bull riders who dismissed them because they knew that the women were getting easier bulls. And she'd get a shot at riding a world-class bull. It could improve her score if her bull was top of the line. But most of all, she could stop the rumor that Mick would spread that Dylan was fixing the outcome of her rides. If he kept his side of the bargain, that is. Still, she couldn't think of a better option at the moment.

"You could arrange the swap without anybody getting in trouble?" She didn't want Dylan to take the heat for this if it went sideways.

"Yeah, they don't keep the bulls segregated. All it would take is a couple hundred dollars to the right person and your bull goes into my chute and vice versa. My guy will switch the names for the announcers and no one else will know about it until the bull is out of the chute, maybe not even then. They'll know once it's over, but then there's nothing anyone can do about it."

"Someone will recognize that they don't have the correct bull in the chute," she said.

"No one cares about that."

"Dylan would care."

"Why? Because he's afraid you'll lose if you're on a better bull?"

LeAnn stiffened. "No."

"Then it shouldn't be a problem, should it? Or are you willing to admit that you can't handle a bull in my category?"

"I can handle the bull. What happens if I don't win this

bet?"

"You admit to me and the rest of male bull riders that girls shouldn't ride because they can't handle a real bull."

Girls? Jerk! "What do I get if I win?" she challenged.

"I'll tell all the boys that we were wrong about you guys. I'd defend you every time someone talks shit about the girls not being real athletes."

She narrowed her eyes at him. "Who cares? No, if I win, you take back that bullshit you said about Dylan beating you up."

"How am I supposed to do that?"

"I don't care. You make it right. Post that it was a big practical joke. Figure it out."

"Sierra Boots still won't touch you."

"Doesn't matter," LeAnn said. "What matters is the truth. So if I win, you're going to come clean."

For a moment, she thought Mick would balk at her terms. But overconfidence must have overridden his doubts because he said, "Deal."

LeAnn held out a hand. "You're going to be a good PR guy for women's bull riding."

"Admitting you're too weak to ride a bull will make my season."

They shook on it.

She knew Dylan was going to be pissed, but she also knew that she could handle any of the bulls in that pen. She had been watching them, studying them. And she had been looking for an opportunity to ride one.

And if Mick stopped his bullshit about women bull riders, it would be worth it. If she could ride this bull, no not if—when—she might be able to lock down another big-name sponsor.

She stayed away from Dylan and the bulls until it was her time to show up for the rides. Mick gave her a nod and she saw the gates slide and her bull was blocked off as another one came trotting up from the back.

Dylan put his hands on her shoulders and gave a squeeze. She jumped.

"Go get 'em, Killer," Dylan said.

She backed him away from the bucking chutes. At his quizzical look, she wrapped her arms around his neck and kissed him. The distraction worked too well because she almost missed her notification.

"I've got to go," she said, breathless from the sweet kisses that took on a gradually more heated edge.

"You've got this."

LeAnn shouldn't have let Mick goad her into this. The bull was an unknown. Hell, all bulls were unknown, until you rode them. But would she have had a better chance to go eight seconds on a "woman's" bull? She had to consider that possibility. She squeezed Dylan extra tight.

"I love you." LeAnn kissed him quick on the lips as he stared at her, stunned.

Not giving him a chance to respond, she hurried to the chute. She did love him. They were in this together. There was no way she was going to lose.

"I love you too," he called after her. She heard him over the roaring of the crowd.

LeAnn was thankful he didn't look like he was going to follow her into the chute, but since she was late, there were already three cowboys in place to help her get settled in on the bull and make sure the ropes were set up correctly. She hadn't wanted to risk that Dylan would stop the ride if he didn't recognize the bull. She had better not blow this. She needed to win, and not just for herself. Because he was going to be pissed when he found out what she'd done.

LeAnn had a moment of trepidation when the bull recoiled and slammed against the chute. But before she could second-guess herself, she tightened her grip and nodded to the gate man.

Chapter Twenty

"LeAnn Keller trying to go eight seconds on Templar."

Dylan's head turned to the announcer's booth so fast, he nearly gave himself whiplash. That wasn't right. Templar was a men's bull. He rushed the gate as he took in the whirling, kicking bull that LeAnn was riding like a champ. A part of his mind could admire the skill, but the rest of him was screaming out in terror. That was not her bull. Had there been an error?

It didn't matter because the woman he loved—who had just told him she loved him—was on two thousand pounds of death. His fingers gripped the railing so tightly, he was surprised he didn't bend the metal. His mouth was dry, his heart felt like it was going to pound out of his chest. It was like Johnny Montana all over again. He kept waiting for the wreck and for that terrible, powerless moment when he'd be too late to stop the bull from stomping on her. But in eight terrifying seconds, LeAnn had jumped free and was on the ground safe and sound.

"What the actual fuck was that?" Dylan snarled, meeting her at the gate.

"Templar was amazing," she said, grinning like a loon.

"I rode him like a boss."

He gripped her shoulders. "I can't believe you were so careless, so stupid. That bull was not meant for you. What happened to the one you picked in the draw?"

"Mick and I switched bulls," LeAnn said.

Dylan closed his eyes, but that didn't help. He couldn't stop the images of Johnny's broken body morphing into LeAnn's in his mind. "Templar was not meant to be ridden by a beginner."

"I'm not a beginner," she shouted at him.

"Yes, you damned well are," he shouted back, his eyes flying open. "We've been riding bulls for ten years. You've been riding them for ten rodeos."

LeAnn took a step back at the vehemence in his voice.

"That bull was larger, stronger and faster than anything you or any of the other women had ever been on."

"And yet I still stayed on for eight seconds," she argued with a vengeance, bumping chests with him.

"You promised me you wouldn't pull this shit anymore."

"All I did was swap out my bull for another one—which is my right as a bull rider," she said.

"You're supposed to swap bulls from the correct pool of animal athletes, not across divisions. And you know that."

LeAnn tried to place a placating hand on his arm, but he shrugged her off. "Dylan, I'm fine. And it's all good. Mick is going to come clean about the bar fight, and he's going to stop being such a douchebag."

"What?" Dylan asked.

"Mick and I made a bet. If I could go eight seconds on

his bull, he'd set the record straight about the fight, and stop causing trouble for me and the other women riders."

"And you believed him? You risked your life for that?"

"I rode a bull that challenged me. My life wasn't at risk."

"What would you have had to do if you lost?"

"I'd have to admit to Mick and the rest of the bull riders that women couldn't handle tough bulls."

Dylan shook his head. "It wasn't worth the risk."

"It was," she insisted. "Besides, he was making noises about you rigging the bulls so that I would win. I had to stop him before we had another internet scandal on our hands."

"It wasn't your place to do that. You shouldn't have done it. It was too dangerous. You're too reckless. You're lucky that you weren't hurt."

"All bulls are dangerous. I could have gotten injured on any bull. Yes, this one was bigger, stronger, faster, meaner—all of that. But I know how to land, and I'm wearing heavy-duty padding. The bullfighters in that arena are the best in the sport. I know I risked a lot, but I didn't do it without thought and I didn't do it just for me. I did it for us."

Dylan drew in a sharp breath. "I can't talk to you right now. That's how angry I am," he said, backing away from her. "I'm not sure I can do this anymore. I can't worry that you're going to pull a Johnny Montana on me."

"What are you saying? You love me. I love you. We just said that."

"And if something had happened, those would have

been the last words you said to me."

It was like he'd splashed cold water in her face. She blinked up at him. "That's not why I said them."

"I can't have you risking yourself to rescue me," he said. "I don't need you to protect my reputation. I could have handled Mick and his rumors."

"I wanted to help," she said. "I saw this as a win-win situation."

Dylan shook his head. "You could have been hurt or worse. How do you think that makes me feel?"

"Nothing happened."

"This time." Dylan gave a half-laugh and then turned and walked away from her.

WHAT THE HELL had just happened?

LeAnn wandered around the rodeo trying to keep the tears at bay. This wasn't how it was supposed to have gone. She had expected him to be mad, but she had thought he would get over it once he realized that the women bull riders could ride the same bulls as the men.

She grabbed a box of popcorn and sat in the stands to watch the men ride. Heartsick, LeAnn watched Dylan's ride. He got tossed off and she knew she was to blame for distracting him before his ride. There had to be a way to make things right again. She didn't want to lose Dylan too.

She did her best not to scowl at the other male bull riders. They had great times on some exciting bulls, which soured her mood even further. Callie and Muriel could have ridden them just as well. When it was Mick's turn, LeAnn watched eagerly, wondering what type of bull he was going to come out riding. When the gate opened, the bull made Fever Dream look like a docile little lamb. Mick was immediately thrown off. He went over the bull's horns and the bull came down on him with its front hooves. It gored him, tossing him into the air. Then it danced around in a circle and landed on him again.

The popcorn box fell from her nerveless fingers as she stood up and screamed. It all happened so fast. The bullfighters tried to get to Mick. The bull kicked a few of them, gouged another one before they were able to lead it out. Mick lay broken and bloodied on the floor of the arena for a long moment, and then he was being lifted onto a stretcher and wheeled out while a horrified crowd looked on.

That had been her bull.

That could have been her.

Chapter Twenty-One

DYLAN FOUND HER in the crowd and crushed her to him. "That could have been you," he muttered into her ear. "Thank God you switched bulls."

She clutched at him, squeezing him tight. "Is Mick all right?"

"They took him to the emergency room," Dylan said. "I don't know what the hell was up with that bull." Dylan wasn't prone to panic, but he felt tunnel vision coming on and he was having trouble breathing. He also couldn't let go of LeAnn. "Please don't get on a bronc today. Please."

She hesitated and then nodded. "Yeah, I don't think I could focus enough to ride right now."

"Do you want to get out of here?" he asked, but he wasn't in a rush to let her go. She was unharmed and alive, safe in his arms. Dylan would get a hotel for the night. They could have dinner and talk this out. He didn't want to be mad at her, especially since her decision to take Mick's asshole bet had saved her life or at the very least, a serious injury.

"I thought you didn't know if you could do this anymore," she said, hurt in her voice.

"I was angry. I'm still angry. But I do love you and I

need to be with you right now to make sure you're all right."

"I rode the damned bull just fine. I want to hang around here until we find out how bad Mick is."

"Dolly can find out for you," he said, letting her go long enough to stare into her eyes.

"I could use a drink," she said grudgingly after a long pause.

Slinging an arm around her, he held her close while he guided them through the crowd to the parking lot. They wound up at a bar just off the highway that also served food. They split an order of fries smothered in cheese and gravy.

"It feels like playing hooky," she said after her second beer.

"Days like this make me wonder if I'm crazy for getting on a bull instead of sticking to bulldogging."

LeAnn shook her head. "Not me. It makes me more determined to keep on riding."

"I used to feel that way," he said. "Until I started picturing myself on the stretcher. Or worse, you."

LeAnn dipped a fry in a pool of cheese. "Ever since Johnny died?"

"Yeah, and now with what happened to Mick, it feels like I'm pressing my luck."

"Was that really my bull?" she asked.

"Yeah, Kingmaker. I saw his stats. He's never reacted like that out of the gate before. In fact, Muriel rode him back in Oklahoma."

"She beat everyone that day," LeAnn said and then

chewed thoughtfully on her fry. "The bull I rode today was tough, but in a different way than Kingmaker. Did anyone do anything to Kingmaker in the chute? Maybe jab him with a cattle prod?"

"I wasn't there, but no one said they saw anything like that." And it would have come out if someone had been playing a prank.

"I don't want to say, 'I told you so,' but this just proves my point. Bull riding is dangerous no matter who is riding the bull. Kingmaker was better than Templar today."

"Better isn't the right word," Dylan said, his head still throbbing.

"You picked Kingmaker for me, didn't you?"

"No. I picked Kingmaker as a bull that was suited for the women's league and not for the men's league."

"Why?"

"Disposition. Past performances. I don't know where I went wrong." He held his head in his hands.

"That's what I'm trying to say. You didn't do anything wrong. At this level, we can all ride the same bulls and we can all either wreck or go eight seconds."

He let out a shaky breath. "It's going to take me a while to come to terms with that."

"Is this going to be a problem for us?" she asked, her eyes beseeching him.

"I don't know," he answered honestly.

When his phone rang, he saw that it was an unknown number. Dylan answered it anyway, glad for the distraction.

"Where are you, Mr. Porter?"

"Who's this?"

"Jackson Blevins. I need to speak with you."

He raised his eyebrows at LeAnn and stood up. "Give me a second to get somewhere quiet."

"This won't take long. I have some unfortunate news for you."

Dylan tossed a few crumpled bills on the table and rose from his seat. "It's about Mick, isn't it?"

LeAnn counted the bills and added some more money before following him outside.

"Indirectly. The WPRC has terminated their relationship with Hickory Livestock."

Dylan stopped dead in his tracks and LeAnn, who had been looking at her phone, bumped into him. "Why?"

"He is being investigated for tampering with Kingmaker."

"Why would he run the risk of hurting his animal?" Dylan asked.

"It's come to our attention that he had placed a rather large bet against LeAnn Keller. If she had lost today, he would have made a substantial amount of money."

LeAnn's jaw dropped. She'd been shamelessly listening in.

An icy cold rage gripped him before the towering inferno of his anger burned through him. "He wanted LeAnn to wreck."

"Did you know about the bet?"

"Yes, but I would never attempt to fix the outcome of a bull ride."

"I believe you," Mr. Blevins said. "That's why I'm only

suspending you for thirty days instead of banning you for rest of the season."

"Thirty days?" Dylan said, his stomach dropping to his feet.

Blevins hung up before he could say anything else.

"I'm so sorry," LeAnn said with a hand on his arm.

"I can't believe this is happening." He dialed Mr. Hickory's number.

"I was just about to call you, son."

"Did you drug up Kingmaker?" he asked, not caring about his winnings.

"I shouldn't have bet against LeAnn. Oh, you're fired, by the way."

"What?" Dylan barked.

"But so am I so don't take it personally. It was nice working with you."

And then Mr. Hickory hung up on him as well.

"Dylan?" LeAnn said. "Are you all right?"

He took a deep breath. He had enough winnings to get him through the thirty-day suspension. He had been counting on Mr. Hickory's salary to get him through the season, though. "I need a minute." Rubbing a hand down his face, he said, "Still no word about Mick."

"Dolly doesn't know anything about him either, but she says that Shelby Miller is calling a Zoom meeting for all the WPRC bull riders in five minutes. Let's go to your truck so we can have some privacy."

They sat in tense silence waiting for the call to start. Dylan did some grim number crunching. He could travel with LeAnn for the thirty days. Or he could try and get a part-time job to fill the time. But he'd need a place to stay that wouldn't cut into his savings. This was a nightmare. He scrolled through websites on his phone trying to find the most cost-effective solution. Dylan had a line on a temporary ranch hand position in Oregon when the Zoom call started.

"Thank you for dialing in, everyone. For those of you who don't know me, I'm Shelby Miller, the CEO of the WPRC. It's been a long day and I'll be brief. Luke 'Mick' Mickleson has sustained a concussion and has broken his collarbone and three ribs. He's in stable condition."

LeAnn sagged in relief, as Dylan closed his eyes and sighed deeply. He didn't like the son of a bitch, but he was glad he wasn't dead.

"The bull that Mick was riding on was one of Hickory Livestock's bulls. Kingmaker was drugged with a substance to make him aggressive. Mick shouldn't have been on that bull. His bull was Templar. LeAnn Keller should have been on Kingmaker today. We're investigating the mix-up. Based on our preliminary findings, we can conclude that someone was trying to sabotage the women's bull-riding event."

There was cross chatter going on and a lot of swearing. Shelby let it continue for a few minutes before interrupting. "The safety of our athletes is paramount. So until further notice, the WPRC has decided to scrap the bull-riding event."

"No!" LeAnn shouted, and she wasn't alone.

"I'm sorry," Shelby said. "We'll revisit it at another time, perhaps next season."

"That's not fair," LeAnn said. "We've all worked too hard. This is a security issue, not a rider issue."

But Shelby had already signed out of the call.

"This is bullshit." LeAnn tossed her phone on the seat in fury.

"Maybe it's for the best," he said, relief making him say things without thinking them through.

"How can you say that?" Her eyes filled up with tears. "Why doesn't anyone believe in us? We can ride bulls just like the men can. Why are we being punished because someone got greedy and wanted to manipulate the outcome?"

"That's not how Shelby meant it. It's a PR nightmare. Ask Dolly."

"I don't want to ask Dolly. I want to ride."

"I'm sorry," he said. Even if he was relieved that she wouldn't be risking herself on a bull, he could empathize with her hurt and disappointment.

"Are you?" she said bitterly. "Isn't this what you wanted? To keep me off a bull."

"I wanted to keep you safe."

"And yet, it's a male bull rider in the hospital tonight instead of a woman. I'm sick of this double standard. It's bullshit."

"Sweetheart," he said, reaching to cup her face, but she flinched away.

"I risked everything for this belt. I took a hit in rankings for bronc and barrel racing so I could excel in bull riding, and now that's all been for nothing because Mick couldn't stay on a drugged bull for eight seconds. How is that fair that the women's event gets canceled?"

"I wish I could help," he said.

"Do you?" And this time her tone was even more bitter. "From the beginning, it was always 'LeAnn, you're not ready.' I was ready. And the irony that's choking me right now is if I had ridden the bull you chose, I would have gotten hurt. I didn't get hurt riding Mick's bull. Why isn't anyone acknowledging that?"

"Because this whole thing is a black eye on the WPRC's reputation. You shouldn't have been able to switch bulls like you did. Kingmaker shouldn't have been drugged, and Mr. Hickory shouldn't have been placing bets on riders who were on his bulls."

"I can't have wasted the last few months for it to end like this. I could have accepted losing. There's no shame in that. But for it to be taken away from us, it's just not right."

Dylan could sympathize. He felt the same away about saving up for the ranch only to have his plans blow up—first when he couldn't get a loan, and now, when he was out of a job and suspended for thirty days.

"Maybe you can talk to Shelby and convince her," he said, but LeAnn was already shaking her head.

"No. Fuck her. I'm going to talk to Jackson Blevins. Give me his number."

Dylan rattled off the phone number. "What's he going to do?"

"You'll see." With shaking fingers, she punched in the numbers. "Damn it. I got voicemail. Mr. Blevins, this is LeAnn Keller. I want to ride bulls for the MPRC. Call me back so we can discuss how this is going to work."

As Dylan gaped at her, she recited her phone number and hung up.

"You can't ride with the men," he said.

"Watch me."

"No, LeAnn, you need more experience on the smaller bulls. It's safer that way."

"I don't need safe."

"That's just what Johnny would say." And now it was his turn to be bitter.

She closed her eyes and leaned her head back. "Maybe I'm the one who can't do this anymore."

Here it was—what he had been expecting all along. But Dylan hadn't expected it to hurt so much.

"You've got a thirty-day suspension, right?" she said, opening her eyes to look at him.

"Yeah," he said gruffly.

"Take that time and really think about if you want to be with me."

"I told you I loved you and I meant it."

"I love you too, but I'm not going to change for you. You're going to have to decide if you can live with that."

Dylan had nothing to offer her. He had no job. No ranch to rescue horses and no future. As much as it hurt like hell, he had to let her go. He would only drag her down.

She opened the truck's door. "I need to be alone right now. We'll talk in a month."

He leaned in and kissed her hard and fast. "Goodbye, LeAnn. Find yourself a cowboy who can take care of you. Not the other way around."

Chapter Twenty-Two

Socorro, New Mexico

LEANN WAS SURPRISED it took as long as it did for her parents to come around. A lot had happened in the past few weeks. The WPRCA was struggling to get fans into the arenas, especially for the events that coincided with times that the MPRC were running bull-riding events with women riders.

She had wanted to compete against the men, but Jackson Blevins was adamantly against it. They compromised by pulling from the same bulls, but the women competed against each other. Both organizations were sponsoring a joint rodeo to take place the first weekend of October in Las Vegas. It would be the first rodeo that Dylan could compete in.

She missed him desperately. Almost every night, she stared at her phone and willed him to call, but he never did. Of course, she could have called him. But every time she weakened, she reminded herself that Dylan needed to put the ghost of Johnny Montana to rest. He'd never be happy with her until he did.

But damn, LeAnn wished he would hurry up about it.

She had gone eight seconds on her first bull and got

tossed on her ass on her second ride. As she was hurrying to get Garth for the barrel-racing competition, she was surprised to see her mother and father in the barn with Reba.

"Hi," she said warily. She hadn't seen her parents in four months.

Her mother rushed in for a hug and LeAnn closed her eyes so they wouldn't see her tears brimming.

"You look good," her mother said, holding her at arm's length. "Tired, but good."

"Thanks," she said. "It's been an adventure. Hi, Dad," she said.

They awkwardly stared at each other.

"What brings you to New Mexico?" she asked. "Is Loretta here too?"

"Loretta's home," her dad said. "We flew out to see you girls."

"Good because that would have been a long drive," LeAnn said.

"It's nothing we hadn't done before, but you're right. Your mother and I are getting too old for the long road trips. It's good to see you." He closed the distance and hugged her.

This time, she did cry a little, but she saw his eyes misting over too so she didn't feel uncomfortable.

"You had a good ride today," he said. "You look stronger than you were at the beginning of the season."

"I had a good coach and I worked hard to improve," she said. She missed Dylan's advice, but she made sure to follow the workouts and the practice schedule that he had created for her before everything spiraled out of control.

"It shows," he said. "We were looking forward to one last family road trip. We're coming with you all to Las Vegas."

Kill me now.

"Vegas is a fun town," LeAnn said after a long pause. "And I'd love to have you in the audience, but I'm already booked at a hotel."

"You can still cancel it," her mother said. "It will save you some money. There's no sense in you eating out and paying for a room when there's plenty of space for all of us in the Winnebago."

Not a chance.

"As much as I miss your chili con carne," LeAnn said, "I've gotten used to being on my own. Garth and I have our own routine."

"Your sisters were supposed to keep an eye out on you," her father said.

"LeAnn can take care of herself," Reba added. "But if she needs me, she knows I'll be here for her. Same as Dolly."

"We're worried about you all alone in Las Vegas," her father said. "There's a lot of temptation in Sin City."

LeAnn smiled. "And I'm sure I'm going to sample all of it. But that'll be after the rodeo. I've come too far to blow it on gambling and booze or whatever else you think I'm going to get into." She hoped her sole distraction would be Dylan, though.

Her parents exchanged a look, but only sighed.

"I've got to get Garth ready for barrel racing. Why

don't we all go out for dinner tonight?"

"Go out? Why? I've got a pot roast in the Instant Pot."

LeAnn's stomach growled. "I'm so there."

DYLAN WONDERED IF LeAnn was looking up at the night sky and thinking of him. He watched every rodeo that was televised, hoping for a glimpse of her and cheered her on from the ranch house after a long day of riding the range fixing fences and herding cows.

"What are you doing out there all by yourself?"

"Just thinking, Aunt Stella."

With nowhere else to go, he'd gone back to his uncle's farm. He knew there would always be work for him there. He got three meals a day and a room in the ranch house. And this time, he was even paid a salary.

It wasn't much, but it helped him to bring Lola home where he could save the boarding fees and keep an eye on her and the rest of the farm animals. No sick or old animal would be sent to the slaughterhouse while he was here. That was a condition of him working at the ranch during his suspension.

"You're going to be late," Uncle Lou said.

"I'm leaving now."

Tonight, he was attending a cocktail party in Dallas. Uncle Lou had gotten him into this event. He had ten minutes to pitch his business plan for the animal rescue ranch to a group of venture capitalists looking to invest in local businesses.

Even though he had been working on his business plan for the last year or so, he was nervous about asking for money. Why should they give him a loan when the banks wouldn't? He didn't even have a real job. Sure, he could return to the rodeo at the end of the month, and there would be large purses for the events. And he had been practicing with Queenie this month. She was no Lola, but she would do the job.

Dylan didn't have high hopes for his chances, but he had to take his shot. If he was ever going to be worthy of LeAnn, he had to have something to his name. But when it was his turn to present his idea for a horse rescue, he nearly froze when he recognized his father on the panel.

Wasn't that a kick in the ass? Leave it to Uncle Lou not to warn him.

His father hadn't ever gotten back to him. Dylan wasn't sure if it was a good sign his father was there or if it tanked his chances. Deciding that there wasn't anything he could do about it now, he launched into his presentation.

When it was time for questions, he wasn't surprised when his father spoke up.

"How are you planning on sustaining the ranch?"

"Through the fees for boarding the horses and other animals."

"Where are you getting the horses from?"

"I have several interested people that I've met during the last few years when I traveled around the United States."

"At the rodeos, you mean."

"That's correct." Dylan remained calm, hoping his

nervousness didn't show in his voice.

"What about veterinary care? How will you budget for that?"

"Through my contacts at the rodeo, I have several vets who I could use in emergencies, and I plan on establishing relationships with the local businesses as well."

His father nodded, but there wasn't anything on his face to clue Dylan in as to how he was doing. Dylan fielded a few more questions from the other investors and just before his time was up, his father said, "I've got one more question."

Dylan waited expectantly.

"Are you going to continue to travel all over the United States to attend rodeos if you receive funding for your project?"

Where was he going with this?

"No," Dylan told him what he had already decided. "The business would have my full attention. I wouldn't be traveling any longer. I still may do a local rodeo or two, just to keep in practice, though." He smiled at the investors and was pleased when they smiled back.

"Thank you, Mr. Porter," the moderator said.

As he was leaving, Dylan caught a glimpse of a few of them frowning over his paperwork and looking from him to his father.

"They'll let you know in writing in two weeks," one of the organizers told him as he was preparing to leave. "Good luck."

"Thanks," Dylan said. He was going to need it.

Chapter Twenty-Three

"VEGAS, BABY," MICK said.

LeAnn ignored him as best as she could. He wasn't competing, thanks to the injuries he'd sustained on Kingmaker, but he'd decided to be there anyway. Just what she needed.

The crowd was huge and the excitement in the air was an almost tangible force. But she was having a hard time concentrating. Dylan wasn't on any of the rosters—not for bull riding or roping or anything. And of course, he didn't call her.

Fuck this. She was going to call him tonight and find out where they stood. This had been the longest month of her life.

Finally, it was her turn to get on the bull. She wasn't paying attention to her surroundings so when a hand helped her get settled, she didn't realize whose hand it was until a familiar voice said, "Give 'em hell, Killer."

"Dylan." She beamed at him.

"Missed you, sweetheart," he said.

"I'll see you in eight seconds," she said.

The flash of cameras and the roar of the crowd was all in the background now. The bull took her on a wild ride, but she kept her seat. When the buzzer sounded, she leapt off. After acknowledging the crowd, she exited and was thrilled that Dylan was right there waiting for her.

Not caring who saw, she leapt into his arms and wrapped her legs around his waist. He kissed her and walked her back to the barn area.

Breathless, he said, "What happens in Vegas, stays in Vegas, right?"

"It better not," she said, easing her legs back to the ground. "Why aren't you competing today?" She didn't move out of the circle of his arms.

"I quit rodeo."

Shock pulsed through her. "What?" Did this mean they were over?

"We can talk more after your second ride."

She grabbed his arms. "Tell me what's going on, but yeah, make it quick. I've got to get back."

He kissed her instead. "It's all good, sweetheart. I'll be here."

"Will you?"

"I'm not going anywhere."

"Good," she sighed and hugged him.

But after her next ride, Dolly intercepted her. "Cowboy Couture wants to talk to you."

"Go ahead," Dylan said with a smile.

"The suspense is killing me," she said, but she was very excited to meet Lila Rogers. She followed Dolly up to one of the boxed seats where the corporations had their own rooms overlooking the arena.

"There she is," Lila said, opening her arms wide when

she saw them. She had large rings on each one of her fingers. After kissing the air on either side of her cheeks, Lila said, "We're so happy to have you on our team."

"What?" LeAnn asked, turning to Dolly in disbelief.

Dolly grinned and presented her with a new shirt. "Surprise!" It was turquoise with white piping and had the Cowboy Couture logo on the chest.

Not knowing what to say, LeAnn blurted, "I'm going to put this on." Dolly just grinned even wider and pointed her toward the bathroom.

She switched shirts and stood for a moment looking at herself in the mirror. She couldn't believe it! She had done it. Cowboy Couture's sponsorship would keep her in gas and Garth in oats for the rest of the season. Now all she had to do was win the whole damned thing.

And find out what the heck was going on with Dylan.

It wasn't until after the barrel-racing competition that she caught up with him again.

"Okay," she said, grabbing on to his arm. "I'm done for a few hours. Let's go back to my hotel room."

"I read about stuff like this happening in Vegas," he said.

"You haven't seen anything yet," she said.

LeAnn hailed a cab, and it whisked them down the Las Vegas Strip to her hotel. She could barely contain her curiosity, but she wanted their conversation to be private and uninterrupted.

But as soon as they cleared the door for the hotel room, Dylan said, "I love you."

And LeAnn figured explanations could wait.

"I love you too. And I missed you so much. Tell me that we're okay."

"We're okay."

"And you can live with me being a bull rider."

"I can live with it as long as you live," he said.

"Deal." She jumped back in his arms, stripping off her new sponsor shirt and bra as he carried her to bed.

"Missed tasting you," he said, tugging off her boots and then her pants.

"You're wearing too many clothes, cowboy," she said.

Clothes flew everywhere until they were naked and pressed against each other. Rubbing against him, she kissed him until she couldn't breathe. What the hell, breathing was overrated anyway.

"Are you wet enough?" he panted, slipping a finger inside her.

She groaned at the contact. "Yes, please."

"I don't think you are." He left the bed, and she slammed her hand on it in frustration, but couldn't resist ogling his fine muscled backside as he grabbed his jeans off the floor and pulled out a string of condoms from his pocket. "Hold these." Dylan tossed them at her, then rejoined her on the bed.

Settling in between her thighs, he passed his tongue over her clit.

"Damn," she screamed, digging her heels into the bed.

He continued kissing her there, licking her intimately until she moaned his name. Sparks of pleasure jolted along her limbs in time with his lapping tongue. She tugged on his hair, moved against his mouth until she had the rhythm that built her orgasm up to a crescendo that froze her limbs and then crashed over her, leaving her shaking and limp.

In the next instant, he sheathed himself in a condom and entered her.

"Yes," she crooned, digging her nails into his shoulders as he sank deep inside her.

Dylan rocked into her hard and fast. She clung to him, legs wrapped around his waist again, so he went deeper and filled her completely with the sweet pumping of his body.

She had missed this, had missed *him*.

"More," she demanded, and he pounded into her faster and harder.

Her moans were loud and echoed in the small room, and the squealing of the bedsprings accompanied her sultry serenade of joy.

"Beautiful, I love you, I missed you," Dylan muttered, his eyes wild and lost in the moment. When he came with a shuddering groan, she quickly followed. They collapsed together in a sweaty heap. She couldn't stop kissing him and his hands were everywhere. He pulled away to change condoms and was back inside her before she could miss him.

This time, he took her slow, all the while kissing her. Her orgasm this time was gentle, but no less shattering, and she clung to him desperately until he achieved his release. They were quiet then, stroking each other and pressing little kisses over each other's face and neck.

Dylan left her briefly to clean up and she might have dozed off, but then he was back, and everything was all right in the world. He held her to him, stroking her hair, and she was content to let him do whatever he wanted to her. He was here and she wasn't going to let him go.

"Why aren't you on the roster for the rodeo?" she asked, biting off a yawn.

"I gave it up, remember?"

Leaning up on her elbow, she looked at him. "Why?"

"A couple of reasons. The biggest one is because I wasn't enjoying myself anymore. After Johnny died, all I could see was death and it was coloring my view of bull riding."

"There are other events in the rodeo," she said.

"Tell that to my knees. But the other reason is because it's a condition of my loan."

LeAnn sat up. "You got a loan?"

He traced his fingers over her nipples, and they tautened at his touch.

"Don't distract me," she said, but she leaned into the caress.

"I like distracting you though." He reluctantly dropped his hand. "But this is important. I went to a group of venture capitalists to see if they would like to invest in my horse rescue farm."

"And they loved it. I knew they would."

"They loved the idea. They hated me. Remember, I have no job history to speak of and even less of a bank account."

"I don't understand," she said.

"My father was one of the venture capitalists I was presenting to. When they turned me down, he gave me a loan under two conditions."

"I don't like conditions," LeAnn said. "Please tell me it's not like Sierra Boots's terms."

"Not a chance. These weren't so bad. The first one was that I had to quit rodeo. And the second one was I had to build the rescue on my uncle's farm. That's where I've been for the last month. Using my uncle's ranch is going to save me from having to buy the property, so I could use the loan money to build the business instead of paying a mortgage."

"Is your uncle okay with this?"

"He is. And I'm glad for a chance to help out the animals on his farm that need it as well. I should have thought of that solution sooner, but I had been too busy trying to do things my way and to be independent of my family."

She traced the hairs on his chest. "Where is the ranch?"

"Just outside of Dallas."

"I'm not going to be seeing a lot of you," she said, feeling a stab of hurt.

"Not while you're traveling, but after the season is over, I'd like you to stay with me. If you want," he said quickly. "I'd understand if you wanted to go home to your parents' house."

"I want to be with you," she said.

"Hot damn, I was hoping you'd say that." He kissed her and one thing led to another again.

Afterwards, she snuggled into him and fought to keep her eyes open. "Are you really sure you're okay with me bull riding? I'm so close to beating Callie and Muriel."

"Trent Campbell taught you well and you learned a lot from my instruction too. You're ready to do this on your own. But I'll always be there to support you and give you advice, if you want it."

"I want it. But what about Johnny Montana?"

"It's time he rested in peace in my mind and soul. It wasn't easy and don't get me wrong, I'll probably have some minor setbacks, especially if you get hurt. But you know what you need to do to succeed, and I'll be there cheering you on, Killer."

"I love you so much," she said.

"I love you too."

Epilogue

One year later

GARTH AND LOLA were grazing in the field when the news broke out that the WPRC and the MPRC had merged in order to stave off bankruptcy. They combined their programs and events into one business called the United Professional Rodeo Circuit of America or UPRC. Dolly was on the fast-track in their marketing division and Reba was one of their top veterinarians. She was currently at the farm arguing with Uncle Lou over which bulls he could send to the events and which had to be quarantined until their blood tests came back negative for performance enhancement drugs.

"You know what this means?" LeAnn said, packing up their picnic lunch.

"Bigger prize money?" Dylan said, reaching into his jacket pocket for something.

LeAnn hoped it was condoms because she was feeling a little frisky. "No, it means I get another chance at winning the first women's bull-riding buckle."

It had pissed her off that the last season she hadn't been able to compete for a buckle while in the MPRC's division of bull riding. They hadn't offered one for the women riders they had picked up on the roster. But what they did offer was a chance to ride more challenging bulls and get in the practice that Dylan and Trent had recommended for her. Now, she felt she could give Muriel and Callie a run for their money.

"You'll do it. I know you will. But before you do, I want to make sure they put the right name on the buckle."

Her eyes widened as he pulled out a ring box.

"LeAnn Keller, would you consider having the name on the UPRC's gold buckle be LeAnn Porter?"

Opening it up, she saw a large square-cut diamond. "Dylan," she said, getting choked up.

"I'm asking you to marry me, Killer. Don't just sit there crying."

"Yes, you idiot. Yes, I'll marry you."

He slipped the ring on her finger. "I didn't think this day would ever come. But you have a way of making the impossible happen. That's one of the things I love about you."

She admired the way the ring sparkled in the sunlight. Then she shot him a mischievous look. "Everyone else is in the front pasture today, right?"

"We're all alone." Dylan grinned at her.

"Good," LeAnn said and pushed him back to the ground and kissed him until they were both breathless.

The End

If you enjoyed *The Cowboy's Prize*,
check out the other books in the

Sweethearts of the Rodeo series

Book 1: *The Cowboy's Prize*

Book 2: *Coming soon!*

Book 3: *Coming soon!*

Book 4: *Coming soon!*

Available now at your favorite online retailer!

More books by Jamie K. Schmidt

Three Sisters Ranch series

Book 1: *The Cowboy's Daughter*

Book 2: *The Cowboy's Hunt*

Book 3: *The Cowboy's Heart*

Book 4: *A Cowboy for April*

Book 5: *A Cowboy for June*

Book 6: *A Cowboy for Merry*

Available now at your favorite online retailer!

About the Author

USA Today bestselling author, Jamie K. Schmidt, writes erotic contemporary love stories and paranormal romances. Her steamy, romantic comedy, Life's a Beach, reached #65 on USA Today, #2 on Barnes & Noble and #9 on Amazon and iBooks. Her Club Inferno series from Random House's Loveswept line has hit both the Amazon and Barnes & Noble top one hundred lists. The first book in the series, Heat, put her on the USA Today bestseller list for the first time, and is a #1 Amazon bestseller. Her book Stud is a 2018 Romance Writers of America Rita® Finalist in Erotica. Her dragon paranormal romance series has been called "fun and quirky" and "endearing." Partnered with New York Times bestselling author and former porn actress, Jenna Jameson, Jamie's hardcover debut, SPICE, continues Jenna's FATE trilogy.

Thank you for reading

The Cowboy's Prize

If you enjoyed this book, you can find more from all our great authors at TulePublishing.com, or from your favorite online retailer.

Printed in Great Britain
by Amazon